# THE CRUDEN [ STOKER ŀ

Adam Drummond's stories

## Adam Drummond & Mike Shepherd (editor)

*(Introduction by Louise Fyfe)*

Supported by The Doric Board

To Ulrike,

Mike Shepherd

# CONTENTS

Introduction By Louise Fyfe

1. Adam Drummond And The Village Of Port Erroll (Mike Shepherd)

2. A Time Line Of Events In Port Erroll Between 1891 And 1895 (Mike Shepherd)

3. Adam Drummond's Stories And Essays

   How The Message Came (Original)
   How The Message Came (English)
   Why Pegsie's Blind Was Not Drawn (Original)
   Why Pegsie's Blind Was Not Drawn (English)
   Hoddie's Grievance (Original)
   Hoddie's Grievance (English)
   A Case Of Conscience (Original)
   A Case Of Conscience (English)
   Stumpie's Proposal (Original)
   Stumpie's Proposal (English)
   The Wreck Of The Pearl (Original)
   The Wreck Of The Pearl (English)
   A Lady Bountiful (Original)
   "Duthie" (Original)
   "Duthie" (English)
   His Lordship (Original)
   His Lordship (English)
   Her Ladyship (Original)
   Her Ladyship (English)
   A Soldier's Daughter (Original)
   A Soldier's Daughter (English)

4. Bram Stoker And The Fishermen Of Port Erroll (Mike Shepherd)

5. What Happened After 1895 (Mike Shepherd)

References

## INTRODUCTION BY LOUISE FYFE

Adam Drummond was my great-grandfather; James Gilmour Drummond was his son, and my grandfather; James Adam Drummond was my father.

I will start the introduction to Adam Drummond's true stories by giving you some background information about my father, who is part of the tale.

My father was a teacher and a historian who wrote stories based on historical events. His attention to detail led him into a constant search for historical details, many of which had been overlooked or forgotten.

For example, he wrote a series of children's books about the adventures of Wallace the firedog, based on the true story of the retriever who helped the Glasgow firemen by running ahead of their fire engines to show them where the fire was. Every fire mentioned in the stories was an actual fire, each one carefully researched and described as close to reality as possible. His earlier book *Cicero the Queen's Drum Horse* was also based on a real story.

My father's research often took us as a family on many an adventure as he sought out possible stories and new finds, including an exciting visit to the royal stables, as well as old castles and graveyards. Throughout his life my father gathered a vast amount of information and his collection of research was immense. Even just before he died, he was still gathering information, writing books and articles, and researching new theories. In particular, he was incredibly interested in Bram Stoker's *Dracula* and had some very interesting views on where Bram Stoker got his ideas for the book.

So when it came to the sad task of clearing out the family home I knew we had a great deal of difficult decisions to make.

Old furniture, books, the family silver and china were all easy to deal with. As a family we either shared what we wanted or left them to be cleared for sale at auction.

But what about the attic? It was full. A neatly-filed historian's collection was not to be seen here; the scene was one of an assorted array of cardboard boxes full of papers, interspersed with boxes of old toys and clothes long gone mouldy or nibbled by mice. In amongst them was an old trunk filled with letters and research which I knew was important, which lay side by side with a box of dollies and pictures drawn by my sister, brother, and I when we were young. On going through one important-looking box I came across a carefully wrapped bundle, only to unwrap it and find a note 'Old Christmas lights – not working'. As I said, my father was meticulous in his attention to detail.

'That's it,' I said, 'from now on we just chuck everything out.'

We didn't quite do that (but almost) and thankfully, when I found the old dusty cardboard box with DRACULA written on the side, I decided to store it in my attic until I had the time to look through it properly. It stayed there for years. It was only when I read Joanna Moorhead's article in the Observer, which mentioned Mike Shepherd and his research into Bram Stoker's time in Cruden Bay, that I remembered the box. I sent the contents off to Mike, and when he quickly got back to me we realised there was an original collection of unpublished stories written by my great-grandfather during his time as Minister in Cruden Bay. And that is really where the story began for me.

This prompted me to carry out some of my own research into my family, and, in particular, to find out a bit more about Adam Drummond. Luckily my father had already done a lot of that research for me and I found it in various boxes, including letters, odd notes, old family photos and other articles of interest. So, here is the story of Adam Drummond's life.

Adam Drummond (1849–1912) started out as an ironmonger, a reforming town councillor in the town of Cumnock in Ayrshire, and a political journalist. He was a friend and political ally of Keir Hardie, who later founded the Labour Party. Both Adam Drummond and Keir Hardie were members of Cumnock Congregational Church as well as being members of the Liberal Party. They both believed that the Congregational movement held the key to a better world for ordinary people, and that the temperance movement, which disavowed alcohol, was an important element in their fight for a better life for working people. During a winter of bitter unemployment they organised unemployed workers into tasks such as cleaning the streets of snow and, in direct defiance of the landlord, the Marquis of Bute, constructed a fishing pond on the River Glaisnock to give the town a clean water supply and efficient sanitation. They paid the workers from the street lighting fund.

Reverend Adam Drummond

In 1889, after a congregational split on the question of discipline, Adam Drummond left politics and went to train as a minister; Keir Hardie left the church and entered national politics. The collection of true stories to follow was written by Adam Drummond during his ministry in the Aberdeenshire village of Port Erroll, which has since been renamed Cruden Bay. This is what my father wrote about them and their relevance to the community:

> Apart from the literary worth of the stories, they build up a composite picture of everyday life in this corner of Buchan more than a hundred years ago and during the years before the building of the railway, the big hotel, and the championship golf course entirely changed the character of the village.

Adam Drummond failed to get the first church vacancy he applied for. In one of his earlier stories he tells why. My father and Adam's grandson picks up the tale:

> During the course of his trial sermon he illustrated a point by striking a match and then extinguishing the flame in a glass of drinking water the beadle had placed in the pulpit. This caused great offence. One of the Elders came to see him in the vestry after the service and gave him the verdict of the congregation.
>
> 'We likit your way of preaching the word of God, he said, 'but we canna' thole the lighting of a match during the preaching.'
>
> The Minister was a little puzzled.
>
> 'Weel, you see, young man,' explained the Elder, 'if we yinst pit up wi' lichted matches in the Kirk, the neist thing wad be caunles an a' the ither geegaws. An there'd be nae end to't.'
>
> ['We liked your way of preaching the word of God, he said, 'but we cannot abide the lighting of a match during the

> preaching.'
> 
> The Minister was a little puzzled.
> 
> 'Well, you see, young man,' explained the Elder, 'if we were to allow lighted matches in the Kirk, the next thing would be candles and all the other stuff. And there would be no end to it.']

The merest hint of Roman Catholic practices in a Protestant kirk was what had appalled the elder.

Thereafter, Adam Drummond became the minister of Port Erroll Congregational Church, where he brought music into the service for the first time. He discussed this with the deacon who seemed to initially favour the proposal. But by the time the minister got round to introducing the idea of a choir and a fund to support the purchase of a small harmonium, the deacon became restive and ill at ease, and was then reduced to hostile silence. 'He sat there,' wrote Adam Drummond, 'looking at me as if I were a fiend of Hell. He swallowed hard and tears of anger sprang to his eyes. In his efforts to control his feelings his face was suffused with rage and then turned sickly green. I formed a very strong impression that this man was not in the least enthusiastic about my suggested innovation. He left without even bidding me goodnight.'

In spite of this unpromising beginning, the Minister put the proposal to the first meeting of the full congregation. To his great astonishment the Deacon was his most enthusiastic supporter. The motion was carried and a few weeks later the rafters at Port Erroll Congregational Church rang to the sound of music. Before long the Minister found out what had gone wrong that night:

> 'It wis a' my fau't. I jist forgot the bittie o' tobacco I wis chawin' until I wis fair settled by your fireside. Then an' feart ye'd be affrontit at my coarseness. So I hung on til't as lang's I could and then I jist swalled it at ae goup. An' oh, Sir, when o got out the Manse yet and doon tae the harbour

wa' I could fair ha,' cried like the Psalmist. 'An' I hinna chawed the nesty stuff sin syne.'

['It was all my fault. I just forgot the bit of tobacco I was chewing until I was very comfortable by your fireside. Then I was frightened you would be affronted by my coarseness. So I hung on to it as long as I could and then I just swallowed it in one gulp. And oh, Sir, when I got out of the Manse and down to the harbour where I could bring it up,' cried the Psalmist. 'And I haven't chewed the nasty stuff ever since.']

It was the same deacon, who in his official speech of welcome to his first church social meeting, introduced the minister by saying how fit he looked now after a few weeks of the fresh breezes and bright sunshine of Cruden Bay. 'He looks a verra fit man noo, but fin he cam to's frae Edinbroo he lookit a bittie like a traaled Haddie.' ['He looks a very fit man now, but when he came to us from Edinburgh he looked a bit like a trawled haddock.']

Adam Drummond grew to love the Buchan dialect and used it more and more in his stories and sketches. According to my father, Adam's Port Erroll writings are probably his best work. He was frequently invited as a guest preacher to distant churches, and was usually asked to read some of his sketches and stories at social meetings in the church hall. On one occasion he was invited to a small church meeting in the West Highlands where the congregation met for their social in the church itself. He read some of his most humorous sketches but there was not a flicker of a smile on row upon row of stony faces. In the vestry afterwards he felt flattened until the Session Clark burst into the room and shook the minister's hand warmly. 'Man, ye were awfu' funny! If it hidnna been that we had been in the Lord's House we could scarce have kept oor faces straight.'

Four generations of the Drummond family: Louise Fyfe / her father James Adam Drummond / her grandfather James Gilmour Drummond / her great-grandfather Reverend Adam Drummond.

# 1. ADAM DRUMMOND AND THE VILLAGE OF PORT ERROLL

Not only did Bram Stoker write *Dracula* in the Aberdeenshire fishing village of Port Erroll (now called Cruden Bay), he also wrote two novels which were set there. Both *The Watter's Mou'* (1895) and *The Mystery of the Sea* (1902) describe the local area as a backdrop to the main drama, with the sense of place further emphasized when his characters speak in the local Doric dialect.

And now it is known that Bram Stoker was not the only one writing about the village at the time. As Louise mentions in her introduction, Reverend Adam Drummond's unpublished stories about the fisher folk of Port Erroll have recently emerged from an attic in Ayrshire to see the light of day. They paint a word picture of a way of life largely gone today - that of a busy Aberdeenshire fishing village.

In Adam's stories we also hear the same fisher folk that Bram Stoker knew as they talk in the Doric dialect. We read about their work, their concerns, and the huge emotional stress suffered by a close-knit community when the fishermen are caught out at sea by a sudden storm. On such occasions this was a group of people much in need of the spiritual support provided by their church minister, Adam Drummond.

The writings of both Adam Drummond and Bram Stoker are the output of two men on a mission: one, a church minister shepherding his flock of devout fisher folk, and the other, an author fascinated by the traditions and superstitions these same fisher folk believed in – many concerning the supernatural. Taken together, the writings provide a unique snapshot of a place, a time and a community: the Cruden Bay (Port Erroll) that Bram Stoker knew.

This book is set out in five sections. The first provides basic information about Port Erroll, followed in part two by a timeline of the significant events in the village between 1891 and 1895: this was when Adam Drummond lived here. In the third section are his short stories and sketches from the period. Mostly written in broad Doric, many will find these stories difficult to read, which is why an 'English' translation has been provided.

Adam Drummond's stories focus on the fisher folk of Port Erroll. Bram Stoker also took an interest in them, and some thoughts about what the fisher folk might have told him are given in the fourth section. Part five provides a brief glimpse into what happened after 1895; the end of the time period covered by this book.

In all of this, do not forget that what you will read about here is a place and a time when work started on a world-famous book – *Dracula*.

The Congregational Church, Port Erroll.

On Saturday, May 23, 1891, a large crowd gathered inside Port Erroll Congregational Church to witness the ordination of their new minister, Adam Drummond. Also present was William Harry Hay, 19th Earl of Erroll, patron of the church and resident of nearby Slains Castle.

Adam, although recently graduated from college, was already

forty-one years of age when he arrived in Port Erroll. Brought up in Old Cumnock parish in Ayrshire where his father was an ironmonger, he started out working in the family business. But then life in the Church must have appealed to him. From 1889 to 1891 he studied at the Theological Hall of the Congregational Churches of Scotland in Edinburgh, and after a short session at the Portobello Congregational Church, he was hoping to start today in his first post as a church minister.

Prayers having finished, the members of the congregation were now invited to put questions to Adam Drummond. In the act of doing so, they demonstrated how the Congregational Church was organised differently from the other established churches in this part of Aberdeenshire, all of which professed the Protestant faith. The Church of Scotland was overseen by a collective of ministers and elected church elders; the Episcopalian Church was governed by a body which includes bishops; whereas each individual church in the Congregational Church was run by the congregation members themselves. And because the members decided everything collectively, they were here today to agree on the appointment of Adam Drummond.

The presiding minister, Reverend Murray from the Millseat Congregational Church in Gardenstown, now announced that, having listened to the prospective minister's answers and in recognition of his record at college in Edinburgh, he would have no hesitation in recommending to the congregation that Adam Drummond be ordained in the usual manner by prayer and the laying on of hands. After short speeches in the church, a celebration dinner was held in the Kilmarnock Arms Hotel, a short walk up the street from the church.

The Kilmarnock Arms Hotel.

The congregation was thereafter happy with their choice. A fellow minister wrote about Adam Drummond that 'He came to them fresh from college with all the zeal of a young minister, and with an evident earnestness of purpose which commanded confidence and respect.' And it was said of Adam Drummond that he was free from 'all narrowness of mind, gentle and charming, yet not afraid to preach vigorously and fearlessly'.

This was a congregation that had been meeting since 1882, having got together because they wanted to conduct worship in the village itself. The three other churches in Cruden parish were not located in Port Erroll or even that close to it: The Church of Scotland is located in the old parish church a mile to the west of the village; The Episcopal Church is one and a half miles to the south-west; and the Free Church of Scotland (now disbanded) was in the village of Hatton, two and a half miles to the west.

The village also held a small number of adherents to an evangelical sect known as the Brethren; it still survives in Aberdeenshire. The Brethren lacked a regular meeting place in the village; one visitor writing that 'it was a usual sight on a fine Sunday evening in the summer to see a congregation of the folk, the women in their curches seated on stools on the one side in front of the line of houses and the men in their Sunday best standing in a row of the other, behind them the estuary of the Cruden Burn and the sand hills, and in the centre of the street a huge fisherman pouring out his soul in a fervent proclamation of the Gospel.'

The members of the Congregational Church on starting out held services for two years in the tiny mission hall built by subscription in the early 1870s as a general purpose meeting place for the village. And then in 1884 a new church was built for the congregation: a simple box-shaped building fronted by a bell tower. William Harry Hay, the earl, granted land for a church building and a manse to house the minister. By 1895 the 'members and adherents' of the Congregational Church had grown to 240 in number. From Adam's stories, it appears that most of the church members were fisher folk from Port Erroll; the earl a notable exception.

When Adam Drummond arrived in Port Erroll the village held 487 inhabitants in 97 houses according to an Aberdeen County Council report. About 300 of the village population were fisher folk.

The geography of Port Erroll at the time was simple - essentially a ribbon development strung out along one side of a half-mile-long road passing along the north bank of the Cruden Water, a stream which runs out into an estuary fronting the North Sea.

At the landward end of this road, where it forms a T-junction with the coastal road from Ellon to Peterhead, is the Kilmarnock Arms Hotel. Listed in an advertisement from the 1890s as containing twelve bedrooms, the hotel catered for holiday makers keen on swimming in the sea in addition to the hunting and fishing set from nearby Aberdeen. The advertisement mentions the trout fishing in the Cruden Water, the sea fishing, and over 6,000 acres of land well-stocked with game. Bram Stoker and his family stayed in the Kilmarnock Arms Hotel on their first three visits to Port Erroll.

Immediately to the south of the hotel lay the narrow granite bridge over the Cruden Water. On the other side was the grain store, mentioned by Bram Stoker in *The Watter's Mou'*: 'the new barn and storehouses Matthew Beagrie had just built on the inner side of the sandhills where they came close to the Water of Cruden'. The date on its front wall still reads 1882.

The segment of village road closest to the hotel was called The Terrace (now Main Street), and further down, after a short dogleg near the Congregational Church, the road became Harbour Street. The fisher folk predominantly lived in and around Harbour Street, whereas the 'tradespeople' lived in The Terrace. Port Erroll was thus a split community both geographically and socially. Within living memory, the two communities were known as the 'down-the-streeters' and the 'up-the-streeters'.

Harbour Street comes to a dead end at Port Erroll Harbour, described by Bram Stoker as:

> ...a tiny haven of refuge won from the jagged rocks that bound the eastern side of Cruden Bay. It is sheltered on the northern side by the cliff which runs as far as the Watter's Mou' [a sea gorge near Slains Castle] and separated from the mouth of the Water of Cruden, with its waste of shifting sands, by a high wall of concrete. The harbour faces east, and its first basin is the smaller of the two, the larger opening sharply to the left a little way in. At the best of times it is not an easy matter to gain the harbour, for only when the tide has fairly risen is it available at all, and the rapid tide which runs up from the Scaurs makes in itself a difficulty at such times.

Adam Drummond's photograph of Harbour Street, Port Erroll.

On the opposite bank of the Cruden Water and its estuary lies the curving crescent of Cruden Bay beach, a wide sandy strand, one and a half miles long, which is backed by an expanse of sand dunes. About a mile down the beach and behind it, is the prominent rocky knoll called Hawklaw. Carry on a bit further, beyond the southern end of the beach, and up onto a path on the cliff-top, and the small hamlet of Whinnyfold is reached with its twenty-three houses. The author of *Dracula* has described this scene:

> The curved shore of Cruden Bay, Aberdeenshire, is backed by a waste of sandhills in whose hollows seagrass and moss and wild violets, together with the pretty "grass of Parnassus" form a green carpet. The surface of the hills is held together by bent-grass and is eternally shifting as the wind takes the fine sand and drifts it to and fro. All behind is green, from the meadows that mark the southern edge of the bay to the swelling uplands that stretch away and away far in the distance, till the blue mist of the mountains of Braemar sets a kind of barrier. In the centre of the bay the highest point of the land that runs downward to the sea looks like a miniature hill known as the Hawklaw; from this point onward to the extreme south, the land runs high

with a gentle trend downwards.

Cruden Sands are wide and firm and the sea runs out a considerable distance. When there is a storm with the wind on shore the whole bay is a mass of leaping waves and broken water that threatens every instant to annihilate the stake-nets which stretch out here and there along the shore. More than a few vessels have been lost on these wide stretching sands and the terror which they inspired which sent the crews to the spirit room and the bodies of those of them which came to shore later on, to the churchyard on the hill. (*The Mystery of the Sea*, 1902)

Cruden Bay beach looking towards Port Erroll.

And this is how Bram Stoker described the lay-out of the village:

The main stream, the Water of Cruden, runs in a south-easterly direction, skirts the sandhills, and swirling under the stone bridge, partly built with the ruins of the old church which Malcolm erected to celebrate his victory over Sueno, turns suddenly to the right and runs to sea over a stony bottom. The estuary has in its wash some dangerous outcropping granite rocks nearly covered at high tide, and the mouth opens between the most northerly end of the sandhills and the village street, whose houses mark the slope of the detritus from the rocks (*The Watter's Mou'*,

1895).

Harbour Street runs down the middle of a hundred-metre wide coastal strip between the estuary of the Cruden Water and a low-lying, flat-topped hill called Ward Hill. Thus the name 'Ward of Cruden', which was given to the fishing village before it became Port Erroll. Adam Drummond, as well as everyone else at the time, continued to refer to the fishing community as 'the Ward'.

Here is Bram Stoker again: 'The village, squatted beside the emboucher of the Water of Cruden at the northern side of the bay is simple enough, a few rows of fishermen's cottages, two or three great red-tiled drying sheds nestled in the sand-heap behind the fishers' houses.' (*The Mystery of the Sea*)

Fishermen's cottages, Port Erroll.

The newer houses, built out of salmon-pink Peterhead granite, are two stories high with white painted dormer windows on the upper floors. It was common for the upper and lower floors of these houses to provide separate dwellings.

The older houses were single-story two-roomed houses generally known in Scotland as 'but and bens'. The 'but' was the kitchen and living room; the 'ben' was the posh room where fancy cabinets held a collection of ornamental plates and chinaware. A small utility room called the 'orra room' separated the two main rooms and was used for storage.

Adults slept in a box-bed in the kitchen. Enclosed within wardrobe-style woodwork and with two doors opening outwards for access, the box bed allowed the adults of the house a degree of privacy. The children slept on the floor or in ordinary beds. These houses were often incredibly cramped – the fisher folk typically raised large families - and in one house in Harbour Street a family of eleven is known to have lived in two rooms.

Bare of carpets or mats, the floors were spread with sand. It was one of the housewife's daily duties to sweep up and dispose of the sand every morning, and to replace it with a new supply dug up from the beach at the edge of the estuary. Adam Drummond describes a floor from one of the houses: 'The sanded floor was plentifully sprinkled with the debris of his repast, for Hoddie followed the custom of the place, throwing the fish bones on the floor after they were clean picked with thumb and finger. As the minister entered Hoddie reached behind him, and, drawing out from the mattress of his bed a stiff oaten straw, began to pick his teeth with it. So long as his mattress lasted, Hoddie would not lack a tooth-pick.'

And elsewhere in his stories, Adam gives a detailed description of the interior of a house in the village:

> The old Pilot lived in a one-roomed house: a little old house with a clay floor trodden hard: a flat stone hearth on which burned a heaped-up fire of coals. The chimney was a hanging one made of a wooden framework attached to the wall and covered over with old sailcloth, well coated with blistered whitewash.
>
> The walls were low, and the dark lines of the rafters

could be traced from wall plate to roof tree. The only ceiling was dried fish lying on the cross beams, and between the lines of fish the bare tiles showed their ruddy sides. A table, a cupboard, a box-bed with doors to shut, three chairs each split across the seat, a little hanging shelf covered with wall paper, on which reposed a few dingy books, made up the furniture. For ornament, a grocer's calendar, a highly coloured chart of the ways of life and death in Chinese perspective, and a Roman Catholic impression in glaring tints of the Adoration of the Virgin, sufficed together with what sunlight penetrated the little square window. From the dusky shadows of the box-bed gleamed a pair of dark, beady eyes, set deep under black bushy eyebrows.

Many of the fishermen migrated to Peterhead in the summer where they were employed catching herring; others fished for salmon, while the rest worked out of the village. They operated twenty or so boats, each about forty to fifty feet long with two main sails. Referred to as small-lines fishermen, they sailed out to their favourite spots within sight of shore, where they caught bottom-living white fish such as haddock and whiting using line and hooks.

The fishermen were distinctive in appearance – to some they seemed almost a separate race. They bore a healthier and more robust physique by comparison to the Aberdeenshire farm workers who worked the land. The fishermen married within the industry and for a good reason too: it ensured that their womenfolk knew what to do; that, and the fact that no other woman would have been interested in the demanding job of a fisher wife. This led to the curious fact that Scottish fishing villages – villages with populations in their hundreds at the time – were mostly inhabited by people with only four or five surnames. As was once said in the fishing village of Newport-on-Tay, Fife: 'Take care what you say about your neighbours at Newport, they are all your uncles and aunties and cousins too.'

The common surnames in Port Erroll were Summers, Milne,

Robertson, Masson, and Tait. Not only did the fisher folk share surnames in common, they only used a small number of first names, typically William, George, or Tom for the men. In a set of stories, which never got beyond first-draft stage, Adam Drummond wrote about three Port Erroll fishermen sharing the first name of William. To avoid confusion, he refers to them as Wullie, Wulsey, and Weelum, adding that, 'their baptismal and surnames were all alike'. This led to the adoption of nicknames by the fishermen, which they knew as their 'tee names'. Adam Drummond commented on the practice:

> Hoddie was once a fisherman, and, like all the rest of the fishermen in the Ward, he had a tee name. Hoddie was his tee name, but how or why he got it I cannot tell. I dare not tell his real name, for he would be offended if, knowing his real name, I called him Hoddie. Nevertheless, should you want to find him in the village and ask for him by his real name, no one will be able to tell you where he lives, but if you ask for 'Hoddie' any 'loonie' or 'quynie' [boy or girl] will tell you.

Photographs of the fishermen from the time show the older men to be mostly bearded. They were dressed in 'pilot-cloth' trousers tucked into their long heavy sea boots and held up by braces. A thick woollen jersey kept them warm and a flat cap or sometimes a bonnet decked their heads.

Port Erroll fishermen circa 1910 (courtesy of Jean Kelman).

| | | | | | | | | |
|---|---|---|---|---|---|---|---|---|
| William Tait | John Summers | Tom Milne | John Hay | George Alexander | William Milne | | | |
| Andrew Summers | George Milne | George Alexander | Robert Taylor | Robert Tait | William McKay | Charlie Mason | G Mitchell | D Mitchell |
| | | Andrew Duthie | George Noble | Alex Robertson | | | | |

| | By-Names |
|---|---|
| William Tait | |
| John Summers | Pad Hulls Jock |
| Tom Milne | |
| John Hay | Jock Lipton |
| George Alexander | George Pot |
| William Milne | |
| | |
| Andrew Summers | Croll |
| George Milne | Boma |
| George Alexander | Geordie Shuner |
| Robert Taylor | Robsie |
| Robert Tait | Robbie Tom |
| William McKay | Tucker |
| Charlie Mason | Coop |
| George Mitchell | Mishak |
| David Mitchell | |
| | |
| Andrew Duthie | Kitly Onzie |
| George Noble | Nobly |
| Alexander Robertson | Gorlin |

Their tee-names (courtesy of Jean Kelman).

The fishermen of Port Erroll took their boats out, weather permitting, to catch nearshore fish using baited fishing lines. Hundreds of metres long, these held hundreds of hooks spaced out at one metre intervals, and were attached to the line by short strands of horsehair.

While the men were at sea, the womenfolk prepared the lines for the following day's work. They collected mussels from the shore for bait, and returned home to remove the shellfish with a sharp knife. Then the lines were untangled and baited for the next day's fishing, a job taking hours. In wet weather the work was done inside the house, and on fine days the women worked together outside where they could be heard whiling away the hours of tedious work by chatting to each other or singing songs together. It was also the job of the women to process the catch and then sell it. In the absence of modern refrigeration, the fish were dried or salted; haddock dried in the sun were known as speldings. The fisherwoman packed the fish into baskets, which were carried on their backs, and then tramped all over North East Scotland to sell their produce in villages or remote farms.

Herring fishery was a large scale operation conducted out of the bigger ports. Although Port Erroll Harbour had been built with the idea of establishing a local herring industry, this ceased after four years. The herring industry was by then concentrated in the larger ports that had a railway station, thus allowing buyers to visit a well-stocked fish market, buy large quantities of fish by auction, and then quickly transport the fish south by rail. Peterhead was one of these. Many of the fishermen in the smaller villages along the Aberdeenshire coast migrated to Peterhead for the summer season, returning on Sundays to see their families and to attend church.

Herring provided a staple item of the local diet. When Bram Stoker opened the Peterhead Flower Show in 1904, he gave a speech. Professing a great love for this part of Scotland, he announced that he hoped to come here as long as he lived and expected to eat herrings all the time. This raised a knowing chuckle.

Baiting the lines, Port Erroll.

## 2. A TIME LINE OF EVENTS IN PORT ERROLL BETWEEN 1891 AND 1895

**1891**

**July:** A group of local businessmen and dignitaries have arrived in Aberdeen to make a deputation to the directors of the Great North of Scotland Railway Company (GNSR). The men were here to lobby the directors with the idea of building a new railway line along the coast between Aberdeen and Peterhead; one that will pass through Port Erroll. This proposal was somewhat hopeful because the GNSR already operated a line from Aberdeen to Peterhead, which after passing through Ellon, proceeded inland to Maud, and from there to Peterhead.

Consider this, the directors were told, significant freight traffic could be expected from a coastal route conveying the produce of local farms, fishermen, and the granite industry, not to mention the income from passengers. The visiting delegation then provided the directors with their estimated volumes of freight and passenger numbers.

Unconvinced that the proposed line would be economic, the directors asked the members of the deputation to go away and check their figures. The meeting lasted an hour.

Later in the month, members of the Buchan Field Club made an excursion to the coast near Cruden Bay, visiting the Bullers of Buchan, a collapsed sea cave, and from there, walking along the cliff top to Slains Castle. Invited inside by the Earl of Erroll, they were shown the drawing room, the dining room, and the library. Club member David Scott talked knowledgeably about the fine art on display, amongst which were two pictures by Gainsborough, and one each by Reynolds and Lawrence. Also in the castle was a dinner set in Worcester porcelain originally made for Admiral Nelson. It depicted Lady Hamilton in various poses as the figure Hope. After Nelson's death, the dinner set was given to King William IV, who later presented it to a member of the earl's family.

There had been an Earl of Erroll living here since 1597, when Frances Hay, the ninth earl, built a tower house called Bowness. Before then, he had been temporarily homeless, on account that his castle, the first Slains Castle, located on the coast five miles to the south-west, had been blown up by a demolition squad personally supervised by King James VI of Scotland. This was Frances Hay's punishment for taking part in a Catholic rebellion.

Slains Castle, circa 1900.

Bowness was substantially extended in 1664, when the building was renamed Slains Castle, and is often referred to as New Slains Castle to distinguish it from what remains of the original Slains Castle. In the 1830s, Slains Castle was rebuilt in the style of a palace by William Harry Hay's father following his marriage to the illegitimate daughter of King William IV (the king had at least ten illegitimate children). William Harry was in effect a cousin to Queen Victoria; his mother being tactfully referred to as the 'natural daughter' of King William.

William Harry Hay took a patronising if somewhat eccentric

attitude to the villagers. The earl would not allow any public house to be opened anywhere on his estate, and the local hotel, the Kilmarnock Arms, was also dry. Visitors complained that when they asked for beer at the hotel on a hot summer's day, they were given non-alcoholic ginger beer instead.

William Harry walked around the village dressed in a tweed suit and a high Glengarry bonnet decorated on the side with a silver falcon brooch. Accompanied everywhere by a large dog, he expected the men to doff their caps to him and the women to curtsey. The earl often struck out at anyone not doing so, being prone to a violent temper. Adam Drummond mentions the earl's quick temper in an unfinished essay, describing how the earl hit a boy who had been staring at him during a church service:

> Wulsey's loonie [boy] cam' hame ae day greetin', an' said at the Earl had strucken him fur glowerin' at him in the Kirk. The neest day Wulsey saw the Earl gyan in by the green gate to the Castle, an' he up to him an' said, quaet kin', 'My Lord, I want a word wi ye.'
>
> The Earl turned sherp kin' on his step an' said, 'Well, Wulsey, what is it you want?'
>
> Wulsey, he says, 'Is't true my Lord that ye strak ma loonie yesterday?'
>
> 'Yes Wulsey, it is true,' said the Earl. 'Something must be done if you do not train your children in good manners. He stared me out of countenance in the church on Sunday.'
>
> 'I'm sorra to hear this, my Lord,' said Wulsey, 'an' sorra to hae to speak to you this wye, but if ony ither man in the Ward had dun't I couldna hae let it pass, an' a daurna let it pass ohn-speakin' wi' you.'
>
> 'Well, well,' said the Earl, 'Teach your boys not to stare at me as they do, and the trouble is over.'

In compensation for his eccentricities, the earl was generous to the villagers. He built a small harbour for the fishermen in 1880 at a cost of between £10,000 and £12,000, provided football and cricket pitches for the villagers, built a reading room, and funded the Congregational Church. He also kept the village rents low and refused to charge rent for widows.

William Harry Hay, 19th Earl of Erroll.

William Harry Hay was thus exhibiting at the end of the nineteenth century the classic behaviour of an English landed aristocrat from the eighteenth century. Back then, a squire expected deference from his tenants, and in return he would generously support them. Between then and the 1890s had intervened the Industrial Revolution, the French Revolution, and the broadening of the voter franchise, all of which substantially changed attitudes within British society. Earl William Harry's behaviour was thus extraordinary for the time; no other local aristocrat in NE Scotland expected their tenants to kow-tow to them like this.

William Harry's wife, Eliza Amelia Hay, Countess of Erroll, known as Lelia to her family and friends, was a woman of great character. She was devout in her religion, open and friendly, and very brave. Adam Drummond and the villagers held her in great respect.

Many years before she accompanied her husband to the Crimean War where he had fought as a Company Commander in the Rifle Brigade. It was said she went to keep a watchful eye on him, even accompanying her husband to his military camp in the field.

Lelia nursed the sick and wounded in the Crimea. A rifleman wrote of her: 'She braves it nobly; she has been under canvas ever since she left England. She is a very benevolent lady. I don't know what the married women would do without her. She is the source of many comforts to them; not as regards money, but of articles that they cannot procure. She fears no danger; where sickness is, there is she.'

While visiting Constantinople, Omar Pasha, Commander of the Ottoman army, gave her a horse, which she named Sultan in his honour. Adam Drummond writes about how Lelia rode the horse around the village. A painting of the Countess of Erroll standing next to the white horse hung in the drawing room of the castle – it was presented to her by the officers in her husband's regiment.

Despite Lelia's close attention, the earl's hot temper got him into trouble with his senior officers in the Crimea, and before any mutterings about a court martial came to anything, William Harry was wounded in the hand at the Battle of Alma (1854). This led to the loss of a forefinger, and he was conveniently invalided back home.

Eliza Amelia Hay, Countess of Erroll (courtesy of Jean Kelman).

**December**: On the first of the month, a legal action was held at Aberdeen Sheriff Court, which was instigated by fishermen from Port Erroll. The plaintiffs were the crew of the fishing boat *Welcome Home*: James Masson, James Summers, William Mackay, William Duthie, and David Alexander.

Their action was against the owners of the Aberdeen steam trawlers *Stephenson* and *Royal Duke* respectively. The men sought compensation of £24 for the damage the trawlers made to their fishing lines, which they had set eight miles down the coast from Port Erroll.

It was alleged that the trawlers, in contravention of the Sea Fisheries Act, had crossed and fouled the fishermen's lines, even though they were clearly marked by buoys at either end. In consequence, the men had lost their daily catch and the lines were damaged.

In turn, the trawler owners stated in court that they had done nothing wrong; that they were fishing outside the three mile coastal limit, and, in any case, no damage had been done. They argued that the fishermen should have known they were setting their nets in the path of the trawlers, and anyway, 'there was no law compelling them to run away at the sight of a fishing boat'.

The court case arose from the long-standing feud between fishermen from the villages along the Aberdeenshire coast and trawler owners from Aberdeen. The trawlermen operated powerful steam ships capable of dragging huge trawl nets behind them to catch large quantities of bottom-living fish; the same fish the Port Erroll fishermen were after.

The waters of the North Sea were already by this time overfished, and the size of the catch dropped year after year, as we shall see. The village fishermen blamed the trawling companies for the decline. Bram Stoker discussed this in his book *The Mystery of the Sea.* In a scene set in Peterhead Harbour, his main character chats to a local fisherman on the quay:

> I had been thinking of the decline of the herring from the action of the trawlers in certain waters, and fancied this would be a good opportunity to get a local opinion… He gave it, and it was a decided one, uncompromisingly against the trawlers and the laws which allowed them to do their nefarious work. He spoke in a sort of old-fashioned, biblical language which was moderate and devoid of epithets, but full of apposite illustration.
>
> When he had pointed out that certain fishing grounds, formerly most prolific of result to the fishers, were now absolutely worthless he ended his argument: 'And, sure, good master, it stands to rayson. Suppose you be a farmer, and when you have prepared your land and manured it, you sow your seed and plough the ridges and make it all

safe from wind and devastatin' storm. If, when the green corn be shootin' frae the airth, you take your harrow and drag it ath'art the springin' seed, where be then the promise of your golden grain?'

William Harry Hay, nineteenth Earl of Erroll, died shortly after midnight on Thursday, December 3. He was sixty-nine.

On the previous Sunday, a stormy day, the earl had been attending evening service at the Congregational Church, and when the service ended he left to visit a member of the congregation. Catching a chill on his way home to the castle, he became very ill later in the evening. Inflammation had taken hold of his lungs, after which there was no hope for him. Yet, up until then, the earl had kept himself reasonably fit. He had installed a gymnasium in the castle which he used every day.

Reverend Adam Drummond closed his sermon the following Sunday by paying a tribute to the earl. Obvious to all in the church was the earl's empty pew, now draped in black. Describing the sight as a symbol of 'a vanished life', Adam said that he had now been minister of the church for seven months and this was the first time he had seen the pew empty. The earl always attended both Sunday services, whether 'in sunshine or storm, in wind or wet'. Furthermore, speaking for both himself and the congregation, he announced that 'we have lost a friend'.

The minister went on to tell the congregation, 'I recall with pleasure the fact that almost his first words to me were "God bless you" and his last words were "God bless you," as he shook hands with me on Tuesday afternoon for the last time. I have talked with him on many subjects – religious, theological, political, social, and historical – and I have rarely met a man with a more exact knowledge of these subjects, or who could give a more intelligent reason for the hope that was in him. He read much, and thought on what he read. He gave a constant study to the Bible, which he quoted with the utmost exactness and appreciation of its meaning; and he keenly relished a quiet conversation on the great question of our "common salvation".'

The earl's funeral was held on Monday December 7, and the memorial service took place within the drawing room of Slains Castle amid much sobbing and tears. At the end of the service, the earl's coffin was carried out of the castle and conveyed to Cruden Parish Churchyard in a magnificent hearse drawn by four black Belgian horses.

Residents from the villages in the earl's estate formed a long procession behind the hearse as it made its way via the castle gardens to the village, proceeding from there to the Erroll Schoolhouse, before turning right onto the road leading to the parish church. At this point the church bell started tolling.

The new earl was Charles Gore Hay, thirty-nine years of age, who apart from mourning the death of his father, was now faced with a large tax demand from the government for death duties. This would have been difficult for him to pay; not the least because income from the estate has fallen considerably on account of a depression in agriculture brought on by cheap grain imports from abroad; that, and his father had been spending but not saving money.

Charles Gore Hay, 20<sup>th</sup> Earl of Erroll (the earl that Bram Stoker knew).

## 1892

**January:** A letter sent from Port Erroll to a local newspaper and signed 'Old Fisher' highlighted the problems facing the fishermen. And again the trawlers were getting the blame. 'When working on the inshore grounds some of our boats had as low as six and ten haddocks a boat for their catch. It has been the poorest season here that ever was seen.' 'Old fisher' notes that the trawlers have been ignoring the three mile limit extending out from the shore: 'We ought to have a Government vessel to protect the fisheries...' He concluded that 'Fishermen cannot live now and keep their families alive on account of steam trawling. Our fishery grounds are finished.'

**February:** On Monday the 8<sup>th</sup>, while the Port Erroll fishing boats were putting to sea at four o'clock in the morning, James Masson, skipper of the *Favourite*, fell into the harbour when pushing off his boat. He was rescued by the other fishermen, a tricky feat in the dark. Such an early start was common for the men, although the time they set off was dictated by the tides; the times of low and high tide changing from day to day. Port Erroll Harbour, a tidal harbour, is almost dry at low ebb, only filling up once the tide starts to rise.

Also in February, on the morning of the 24$^{th}$, disaster visited Port Erroll when the French schooner *Perle* (Pearl) hit a rock near the harbour. Her masts toppled over killing two men. Thereafter, the ship drifted off and became stranded in shallow water just beyond the beach. This should have been a routine rescue mission for the men of Port Erroll. However, all went horribly wrong. The French sailors, unfamiliar with the rescue procedure, panicked, and three of them drowned in the sea (Adam Drummond provides an eye-witness account of the disaster in his essay 'The Wreck of Pearl', which can be read later in the book).

**May:** In view of the forthcoming General Election in July 1892, Colonel Russell, the Conservative and Unionist candidate, gave a campaign speech in the Mission Hall on the third of the month. The main issue of interest, as always, concerned the activities of the trawlers. Recognising the great bitterness caused, he pointed out that the present Conservative government had been responsible for establishing the three-mile exclusion limit along the coast for trawlers, and had increased the penalty for illegal fishing inside it from £5 to £100. He too was concerned that not enough was being done to police the trawlers activities, and had been told that on the previous Sunday nine steam trawlers were spotted within the three mile limit offshore from the nearby village of Boddam. He favoured more stringent measures being put in place. To great cheers, he proposed that such measures should include the confiscation of the nets from any trawler found breaking the law.

**June:** George Cruickshank, the proprietor of the Kilmarnock Arms Hotel, was killed on Sunday, June 25. His horse-drawn gig overturned while negotiating a sharp turn in the road while returning from Ellon to Port Erroll. George was thrown out of the gig, only to land in amongst the horse's feet as it attempted to free itself by kicking out. Suffering severe internal injuries, he died the next day.

George, who started out as a farmer, had taken over the lease of the hotel when it was built in 1878. The following year, a Post Office was opened in the building and George also became the postmaster. Back then the incoming mail was hand-carried from Ellon to the crossroads at Forvie where the Collieston road branches off, and then handed over to 'Postie' Watt. From there, he delivered and collected mail from houses along the way, arriving on foot at Port Erroll at 2 p.m. 'Postie' Watt then returned with the outgoing mail, walking to Collieston where he dropped off the mail with the sub-postmaster for dispatch to Ellon at 5 a.m. the next day. 'Postie' Watt thus walked a round trip of sixteen miles, six days a week, for which he was paid a weekly wage of 12 shillings.

A few years later, the Ellon office acquired a mail gig, which passed through Port Erroll at 11 a.m. and returned to collect the outgoing mail at 3 p.m. And in 1880 a Telegraphic Office was also opened in the hotel, a service which Bram Stoker frequently used.

George's oldest son James Cruickshank took over the hotel. Although George was effectively bankrupt when he died - no matter - James Cruickshank, adept at everything he put his hands to, including business, soon paid off the debts.

James Cruickshank (courtesy of the Kilmarnock Arms Hotel).

**July / August:** Bram Stoker made his first visit to Port Erroll this year. His biographer Harry Ludlam writes that this happened in 1893, although according to the *Buchan Observer* newspaper in an article written closer to the time the first visit took place in 1892 (which is more likely).

A gossip columnist in the *Buchan Observer* (26/10/1897) gave an account of how Bram Stoker discovered the area:

> Cruden has an enthusiastic friend in Mr Bram Stoker, Sir Henry Irving's manager. Mr Stoker (says a London correspondent), made the acquaintance of the district – as he tells me – by accident. He wanted to find a bracing place far north on the east coast. From a large ordnance map and the geological formations, he knew that some such place

must lie between Peterhead and Aberdeen.

Accordingly he went to Peterhead and walked down the coast, and when he saw Cruden he telegraphed to his family to come on to the Kilmarnock Arms Hotel. Mr Stoker has been there every summer since then, and hopes some day to have at Cruden his own *pied-a-terre*.

Bram Stoker never explained any of this; and his diaries or notebooks from the era have not survived either. One can only guess what he had been thinking. Perhaps he sought a regular holiday spot to write his books and at a far enough distance to make it impractical for his demanding boss, the famous actor Henry Irving, to call him back to London on a whim.

I also suspect that a desire to find a regular writing spot was prompted by the death of the American poet Walt Whitman in March 1892. If Walt Whitman was the master, Bram Stoker was his ardent disciple. Even today it is not fully appreciated by the literary world just how many allusions to Whitman's poetry are to be found in Bram Stoker's writings. Bram would have been devastated by the death of his guiding light, perhaps to the extent of making a conscious decision at the age of forty-four to systematically pursue his ambition to become a literary man. To judge by his regular output of books after 1892, his discovery of a regular writing locale at Port Erroll made a big difference.

The characters in Bram Stoker's stories appreciated the charms of Port Erroll and the surrounding area: The family members in his short story *Crooken Sands* (1894) 'had never seen so delightful a spot. The general satisfaction was more marked as at that very time none of the family were, for several reasons, inclined to find favourable anything or any place over the Scottish border.'

And from *The Mystery of the Sea* (1902): 'When first I saw the place I fell in love with it. Had it been possible I should have spent my summer there, in a house of my own, but the want of any place in which to live forbade such an opportunity. So I stayed in the little hotel, the Kilmarnock Arms. The next year I came again, and the next, and the next.'

Bram Stoker did indeed return year after year. There is evidence for at least twelve visits, typically a month at a time, and on a thirteenth occasion (1896) he was in Aberdeenshire but with no record that he came to Port Erroll that year (although he probably did).

**September:** It is rumoured that the Great North of Scotland Railway Company were now seriously considering building a new railway line from Ellon to Boddam via Port Erroll (although it is not known today why the proposed line stopped short of Peterhead, which lies four miles beyond Boddam). Officials from Peterhead Town Council reckoned it absurd that the proposed line did not go the full way, noting, for example, that the fish from Port Erroll was presently being transported to Peterhead by 'an old white horse'.

**November:** The Ellon District Committee of Aberdeen County Council met on November 2, and public health was on the agenda. There was much to be improved in the district, not the least because within the last sixty years there had been two major outbreaks of cholera in Aberdeenshire, an infectious disease that thrives in insanitary conditions. In 1866, 46 people died from cholera in Fraserburgh, and 32 from the village of Collieston in 1832.

Much concern was expressed about the unhealthy conditions in Port Erroll. In the upper village, privies were connected to 'ashpits', holes in the ground for the disposal of ash from the hearth and household waste. The committee reported that there were 'a good many imperfect ashpits in this place with stagnant water causing very bad smells. There is a slaughterhouse here which ought to be removed to a greater distance from the village, as it is too close to the houses and not at all well kept.' The recommendation was made that, to start with, household waste should be removed by a scavenger, whose job would also include sweeping up horse manure from the village streets.

The Medical Officer also added his bit, saying that the ashpits were in the worse condition he had ever seen, that every single one in the village was 'nothing but a reeking cesspool'. Part of the problem was the blockage or absence of drains to carry away the slop water.

Not mentioned in the Council report was the method of sanitation in the fishing village. The houses did not have toilets inside or outside (a state of affairs persisting up to the 1950s). Bodily needs were supplied by 'gizunders' - large china bowls that 'giz' under the bed. These were emptied into a large 'accommodation' bucket kept just inside the front door of the house. A daily household chore of the fisher wife was to carry these buckets down to the shore of the Cruden estuary and empty the buckets onto the sand. The footpaths connecting Harbour Street to the shore for the purpose still survive.

The fishing village of Port Erroll must have been an exceptionally smelly place in the 1890s. In addition to the aroma of sewage, a lingering smell of fish and coal smoke hung over the village. Bram Stoker also mentions a rubbish tip of fish offal and household refuse near Port Erroll Harbour. What is curious about all of this is that apart from a fleeting reference in a gazetteer describing Port Erroll as a dirty village, there are no contemporary reports which mention the smell of the place. I suspect that few at the time would have found the observation worthy of comment, because Victorian towns and villages were probably all somewhat pungent.

Victorian pump, Harbour Street.

Yet another issue was the inadequate water supply, particularly for the fisher folk. Water was piped from a field one and a quarter miles inland to the upper village, and what was left over then fed to tank on a hill to provide the supply for the fishing village. From here, it flowed through lead pipes to pumps located along Harbour Street (two still survive).

The Council report noted that the water supply 'was very deficient, especially when the fishermen are all at home. This deficiency has led on one or two occasions to water riots. On one of these the fishermen cut off the supply to the upper village, being determined that their neighbours should not enjoy a supply.'

Also this month, William Summers, fisherman from Port Erroll, had a letter published in the November 15th edition of the Peterhead Sentinel newspaper. Headlined 'The Trawling Question', William discussed the proposal to close the Moray Firth to trawlers, and took issue with protests by the trawling interests in Aberdeen opposed to the idea. Although the trawling lobby is all powerful, William hopes that reason will prevail.

He speaks as one of those arrogantly dismissed as 'ignorant fishermen like the lonely mariner who perishes at sea, our cry being unheard'. Matters must change, he argued, otherwise '47,000 fishermen if not by a power guided by a scientific knowledge, will be by the power of humane feeling and affection caused to throb in their breasts by the wants of their starving families make Scotland tremble and shudder at the injustice done to them...'.

In 1892, four ports on the east coast of Scotland were licensed for trawlers: Aberdeen, Montrose, Anstruther, and Leith. The total number of trawler boats at these ports, particularly Aberdeen, increased year by year. What William Summers described as the great industry of line fishermen and herring netters in the fishing villages on the east coast 'is going to be lost to our country through the destructive act of trawling'. He would like to see the three mile limit further extended offshore; some suggested a twenty mile limit, which he supported. Otherwise, 'If things continue as they are many an honest, industrious, sober-living family will be starved to death.'

**December:** The Dowager Countess of Erroll, Eliza Amelia Hay, left Slains Castle to take up permanent residence in London. The law allowed her as a widow to retain her late husband's place of residence for a year after his death, and with the year having gone by, the ownership of the castle had passed to her son, the current earl. Queen Victoria now graciously granted her the use of Cambridge Cottage on the west side of Kew Green in London. For many a year, Leila had acted as a lady-in-waiting to the queen, and was frequently in her company.

The appeal made by the owners of the trawlers *Stephenson* and *Royal Duke* against the £24 damages awarded against them in favour of the Port Erroll crew of the *Welcome Home* was rejected by the Court of Session. It was decreed that the trawlermen had not taken proper precautions to avoid the fishing lines set by the Port Erroll men and, in any case, the trawlers only have rights to the sea if it is unoccupied at the time.

This month, the Fishery Board published figures showing that the total value of the fish landed on Scottish coasts for the first eleven months of 1892 was £1,582,329, a decrease of £158,324 (9 per cent) from the same period in 1891.

## 1893

**January:** 1,500 fishermen took part in a huge demonstration against trawling in Peterhead on January 28, the largest of its kind. Hundreds marched in procession through the streets of the Aberdeenshire port accompanied by pipers and flute players. A lorry led the procession, carrying a fishing boat complete with a crew shooting and hauling their lines. On the mast of the boat was nailed a placard with the words: 'No fish here'.

At a meeting held in parallel with the demonstration the first resolution made asked the Government to review the practice of beam trawling. That is, where a heavy-duty net is held open at its mouth by a steel or heavy wood beam and then dragged along the sea bed by the steam trawler; the intent to catch bottom-living fish, commonly known as white fish. One attendee spoke for all present, 'We view with alarm the rapid diminution of all kinds of white fish round the Scottish coast, which we feel is mainly attributable to the system of beam trawling, which destroys the spawning grounds, and captures large quantities of small and immature fish...'

Another speaker reviewed the growth of the trawling industry on the east coast of Scotland. There had been 43 trawlers in operation in 1883 and 132 trawlers in 1891, a threefold increase in eight years. A total of 95 trawlers landed fish at Aberdeen in 1891, of which 37 were Scottish owned and 58 English owned.

These trawlers were believed by the fishermen to have caused a rapid depletion of the fishing grounds on the east coast of Scotland. And not just on this part of the North Sea either. It was mentioned that an international conference held in 1890, attended by representatives from Germany, Holland, Denmark, and France, had proposed that statistics on fishing catches should be collected as the basis for instigating an international agreement to regulate fishing in the North Sea.

Alexander Duthie from Port Erroll also spoke, complaining that given the practice of Sunday trawling it was a wonder that judgment did not come down upon the trawlers breaking the Lord's Day.

The protest and meeting in Peterhead led to the circulation of a petition signed by 9,800 fishermen. It asked the Secretary of State for Scotland to convene an international conference to establish the cause of the 'great decrease which continued to take place in the number of food fishes frequenting the Scotch fishing banks, and if it were found due to trawling, to prohibit the practice of that injurious mode of fishing, and also to provide a more efficient sea police for the purpose of enforcing regulations with regard to beam trawling'.

**March:** The Port Erroll Literary Society met every week, and, in one of its sessions in March, Mr Bruce read an essay on the best methods of spending leisure hours. He was introduced by the president of the society, Reverend Adam Drummond.

Not that the villagers needed any lectures on how to spend their spare time. If they so wished they could join a dramatic society, a self-improvement society, several athletic organisations, and others aside. The Earl of Erroll, when he was in residence at Slains Castle, also gave woodwork lessons to the villagers.

**April:** The directors of the Great North of Scotland Railway Company took their horse-drawn gigs for a drive along their proposed railway line this month, stopping off at Port Erroll to select the site for a new hotel. Afterwards, they were entertained to lunch at Slains Castle.

**May:** The Earl of Erroll has sold the dinner set depicting Lady

Hamilton as the figure Hope. It is an early sign of the money difficulties facing the owner of Slains Castle.

**July:** A select committee of the House of Commons in London started an enquiry into the Scottish sea fisheries this month. It will hear from witnesses representing all concerned parties.

In the session held on July 13 the committee heard evidence from representatives of the fishing industry in Aberdeen. First up was John Freeland, a line fisherman from Torry, a village located just south of Aberdeen. He believed that his fellow fishermen had been more affected by trawlers than any other Scottish port given that Aberdeen was the centre of the trawling industry. The trawlers operated every day of the week 'including the Sabbath'. And once one fishing ground was played out 'until there was hardly anything left', they moved on to another one. They were relentless; showing no respect for the immature fish caught in their nets or by trawling over the spawning grounds. A relation, who had once worked on a trawler, told the fisherman that 'his heart was sore when he had to take the shovel and shovel the small fish overboard'. Noting that haddocks spawned from the beginning of February to mid-March, he recommended that trawling should be prohibited at this time, but so should line fishing, although he was aware that this would be hard on the men involved.

Next up was 'Baillie' William Pyper, manager of an Aberdeen steam trawler company operating ten boats out of the port. He told the committee that he was 'practically the originator of the trawling industry at Aberdeen about ten or eleven years ago'. His boats caught very few immature fish, he said, and they landed all the fish they caught. The success of trawling in Aberdeen had been responsible for a decrease in the number of boats run out of nearby fishing villages on account of the better market in the city and the ease of dispatch from its railway station.

Pyper reckoned that there had been no decline in the catch made by line fishing in Aberdeenshire, and stated his theory that trawling was actually beneficial for it. That's because the trawlers catch the monk fish, dog fish, and sharks that prey on other fish species. He reckoned that 'every one of our trawlers would have not less than have a ton of these monsters, and he supposed that were no less than 1,500 tons of these caught annually and sold for manure'. Furthermore, if the Aberdeen trawling industry was hampered even more than it had been, at least £70,000 to £100,000 worth of fish would never reach Aberdeen. He also noted that trawling activities out of Aberdeen now extended to Orkney, the Faroes, and Iceland.

In response to the evidence provided by William Pyper, Mr Kearley, a member of the Commons Committee of Enquiry, said that, 'It is quite refreshing to hear somebody who is prepared to support trawling, and to give reasons for doing so.'

Kearley's comment is an indication of how the trawling industry was supported by many politicians of the day: the British population had increased substantially since the Industrial Revolution, and for the large numbers of working class men and women living in the cities of Victorian Britain fish provided a cheaper source of protein than meat.

On July 20, the committee heard evidence from Alexander Duthie, who was representing the fishermen from both Port Erroll and the nearby village of Boddam (Adam Drummond writes about Duthie's visit to London in one of his stories).

Alexander Duthie talked about the decline in the fishing catch from the sea near Port Erroll. Back in 1870, he habitually shot a fishing line on a Saturday night, and, on retrieving the line on Monday, it held between 300 and 400 fish. By 1878 this had reduced to a typical catch of 300 fish. And today in 1893 he could put twelve lines in the same stretch of water 'and he would not get one half of the number that he used to get on one line'. He recalled that when he was a boy, old men would lay a baited line along the rocks at the water's edge at low tide, and 'letting the tide cover it, get from 10 to 12 score of large haddock and any amount of cod, turbot, and plaice. Today, these parts were cleaned.'

In his view, the exclusion zone for trawlers should be

extended to between ten and twelve miles from the coast. He countered Baillie Pyper's assertion that trawling improved line-fishing. If so, he argued, why were these trawlers going as far as Iceland to catch fish? In truth, these trawlers were being allowed to do exactly as they liked.

He was aware that the Fishery Board for Scotland had been given the services of HMS *Jackal* to police the activities of trawlers. He had never seen the ship, nevertheless he had been told that they had 'taken a trawler or two in Aberdeen Bay'. Yet, much more was urgently required to police the activity of the trawlers.

---

**— PORT ERROLL. —**

## KILMARNOCK ARMS HOTEL,

On the Line of New Cruden Railway.

### Port Erroll, . . .
### ABERDEENSHIRE.

TELEGRAMS:
"KILMARNOCK ARMS,"
PORT ERROLL.

OBJECTS OF INTEREST IN THE VICINITY—
SLAINS CASTLE, OLD SLAINS, BULLERS O' BUCHAN, DUNBY ROCK, AND OTHER GRAND ROCK SCENERY.

THIS HOTEL contains 12 Bedrooms, 2 Bathrooms (hot and cold water), Sitting Rooms, Dining Hall, etc.; and is admirably adapted for small parties or families. Excellent Bathing Beach within seven minutes' walk; Bathing Houses for use of Visitors. Terms Moderate. Families and Parties can have special terms by arrangement. No charge for attendance. All Visitors may have Trout Fishing in Cruden Water free of charge. There is good sea Fishing, and boats may be had for hire; also a good Golf Course. The proprietor is Lessee of over 6000 acres of Shooting (well stocked with low ground Game, which includes a small Grouse Shooting. Gentlemen residing at the Hotel may have Shooting by previous arrangement, with use of dogs, etc., on reasonable terms. Horses and Machines kept for hire.

POSTAL AND TELEGRAPH OFFICE IN THE HOTEL.

JAS. CRUICKSHANK, *Proprietor.*

---

**July / August:** It's unlikely that Bram Stoker visited Port Erroll this year. The Lyceum Theatre Company embarked on a North American tour in August and Bram Stoker went with them. As the business manager for the theatre he was responsible for organising everything, and he probably did not have much time to do much else that summer.

**September:** A scavenger had been appointed by the council to remove manure and refuse from the village. On the face of it this looked to be an ideal arrangement because the scavenger worked free of charge to the council - he used the products of his diligent gathering for his market garden. Even so, some of the villagers have protested, arguing that they were not being paid for what they considered to be the taking of their property. Only a few spoke up on the matter, but had influenced the others. In disgust, the scavenger resigned the post. The council now considered the possibility of prosecuting the villagers should they not cooperate once a new scavenger is appointed.

**November:** More details emerge about the hotel to be built at Port Erroll. It will be 'palatial' and a golf course will be built on the sand dunes behind Cruden Bay beach.

**1894**

**February:** A meeting is held in the Mission Hall to discuss building a public hall in Port Erroll. Recognising that a hall was needed for public meetings and entertainments, the meeting unanimously approved the proposal and a fund-raising committee was appointed.

**July:** During the digging of a trench for the new water supply, a large quantity of human skulls and bones was unearthed. These were discovered in an ancient churchyard located on a knoll on the opposite bank of the Cruden Water from the Kilmarnock Arms Hotel. The St Olaf's Church that once stood on this spot had been named after the Patron Saint of Norway and Denmark; the tradition being that it was built following the Battle of Cruden Bay between the Vikings and the Scots in the year 1012. Many believe the uncovered remains to be those killed (modern historians state that the evidence for the Viking battle is anecdotal only - although it might have happened – the problem being that there is hardly any surviving documents from the time to say yay or nay definitively).

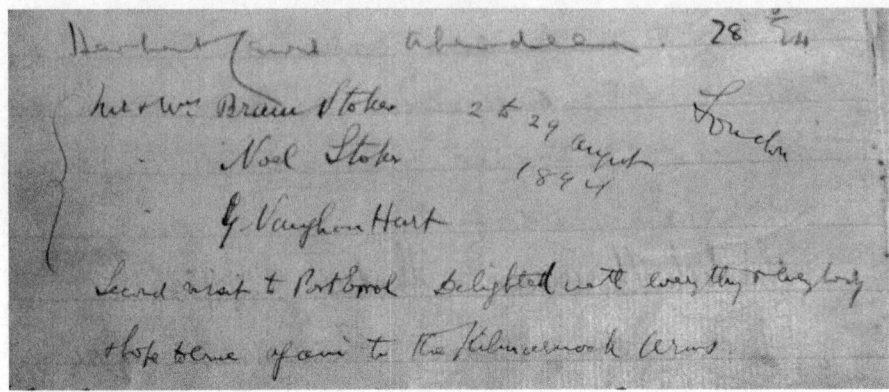

Bram Stoker's signature in the Kilmarnock Arms guest book, 1894.

**August:** Bram Stoker, his wife Florence, and son Noel arrived in Port Erroll on August 2 and booked into the Kilmarnock Arms Hotel. They will stay until the 29th. Also with them was Bram's friend George Vaughan Hart, Professor of Law at Trinity College Dublin. Bram signed the guest book, 'Second visit to Port Erroll. Delighted with everything & everybody & hope to come again to the Kilmarnock Arms.'

On his visit this year, Bram was probably hoping to complete his novel *The Shoulder of Shasta*, a love story set in the California wilderness. He will also be thinking out the plot for his first Port Erroll-based novel, *The Watter's Mou'*.

If Bram had been walking along the coast on Wednesday, August 22 he would have witnessed a spectacular sight. A huge school of whales was spotted swimming packed together three miles offshore from Slains Castle. They were splashing their fins and blowing their spouts - all in all making such a big racket they could be heard over several miles.

The grain store, now Cruden Bay Garage.

A gala to raise funds for the new village hall was held in the grain store on August 25, and the Stoker family turned up for the occasion. On doing so, they would have noticed that this somewhat drab, functional building had been brightly decorated outside with colourful flags and banners. And having gone inside, the walls were seen to be covered with flags of all nationalities, the pillars draped with muslin of different shades, and Chinese lanterns hung from the roof. On sale at the ten stalls laid out on the upper floor were flowers, toys, china, dairy produce, fish, refreshments, and jumble. Elsewhere in the building could be found an art gallery, wheels of fortune, and an air gun shooting range in the charge of Sergeant-Instructor Thomson from Hatton.

Charles Gore Hay, 20th Earl of Erroll, in his first public appearance since the death of his father, opened the bazaar with a short speech at 11.30 a.m. A large crowd jam-packed the building with hardly any space to move. The final takings for the bazaar were £160, which in addition to the £70 already raised put the overall funds for the new hall at a figure not far short of the target £300.

The event was later transformed by Bram Stoker into a scene in his novel *The Watter's Mou'*, where it became a wedding ceremony. And curiously enough, some of the real–life attendees listed as attending the bazaar were also at the fictional wedding, including James Beagrie, William Macpherson, David Mitchell, John Reid, and James Cruickshank.

Here is how Bram Stoker described the wedding scene in *The Watter's Mou'*:

> There appeared to be little rivalry between the two shoemakers, Macpherson and Beagrie, who chatted together in a corner, the former telling his companion how he had just been down to the lifeboat-house to see, as one of the Committee, that it was all ready in case it should be wanted before the night was over. Lang John and Lang Jim, the policemen of the place, looked spruce ever than usual, and their buttons shone in the light of the many paraffin lamps as if they had been newly burnished. Mitchell and his companions of the salmon fishery were grouped in another corner, and Andrew Mason [Masson] was telling Mackay, the new flesher, whose shed was erected on the edge of the burn opposite John Reid's shop, of a great crab he had taken that morning... Just then two persons entered the room, one of them, James Cruickshank of the Kilmarnock Arms...

## J. BEAGRIE,

### Boot and Shoemaker,

CRUDEN BAY, PORT-ERROLL,

Has always on hand a Large Selection of

### Boots, Shoes, and Slippers,

Of Every Kind and Size.

GOLFERS' BOOTS AND SHOES
A SPECIALITY.

Every Requisite in the Shoe Trade kept in Stock.

---

PORT ERROLL.

# JOHN REID,
### Draper and General Merchant.

*Jackets, Mantles, Capes, and Waterproofs.*

The Latest Novelties in Millinery and Fancy Goods.

A Choice Selection of the Finest TOBACCOS, PIPES, and TOBACCO POUCHES.

GLASS, CHINA, AND GENERAL IRONMONGERY.

Dressmaking, Millinery, and Ready Mades.

---

**September:** A severe gale blowing from the north lashed down the Aberdeenshire coast on Friday 7th. The fishing boats, which had gone out on the previous day, and several on Friday, had not returned home by late Saturday night. Some sought shelter in Aberdeen, and a Buchanhaven drift netter took refuge in Port Erroll Harbour having lost all her nets. This is probably the storm mentioned by Adam Drummond in his stories as having caused much anxiety in the village. Even so, this was a relatively minor blow-up by comparison to North Sea storms within recent memory: in October 1875 an estimated 15 vessels and fifty six lives were lost off the Scottish coast, and in December 1876 an estimated 31 vessels were lost with at least 150 deaths.

The Public Hall committee met on September 7, and, estimating their funds to now stand at £275, approved a decision to go ahead and build the hall. A building committee was established to move the project forward.

On Saturday 8$^{th}$ the new Ellon to Boddam railway line was inaugurated by the Countess of Erroll at Ellon Station when she took a little silver-plated spade, cut the first sod of earth, and placed it as directed into an oak wheelbarrow. Wheeling it along a wooden walkway, she tipped the earth onto the field where work was imminently due to start on the project. This unlikely labourer was wearing a green satin mantle with jet trimmings, a black satin dress, and a hat with black feathers. When complete the line will run fifteen and a half miles from Ellon to Boddam, with stations along the way at Auchmacoy, Pitlurg, Hatton, Port Erroll, and Longhaven.

The weather still being unsettled, the dignitaries did not hang around outside for too long. After a short trip they arrived at the grounds of Ellon Castle where a celebration luncheon was held for them in a marquee erected on the lawn. In the speeches to follow, the Earl of Erroll applauded the new line because it would now bring Port Erroll within twelve hours travel time of London. The Managing Director of the railway company also spoke, reckoning that by the time the project was completed in two years time, Port Erroll would then be in a position to boast about a hotel he would make 'the most extraordinary, beautiful, and perfect in Europe'.

The Cruden Bay Hotel in 1912. It was demolished in the 1950s.

On Friday, September 21, Tom Morris, professional golf player and course designer from St Andrews, visited Port Erroll to lay out the golf course on the dunes next to the proposed hotel site. Work on the course was expected to start soon.

**October:** On October 10, the steamship *Chicago*, en route from Sunderland to Baltimore, ended up on the rocks directly under Slains Castle. Although the ship had set off in good weather, a gale blew up that night. As the vessel passed around the Cruden Skares into the Bay of Cruden at twenty to one in the morning, a combination of a strong ebb tide and a southerly gale-force wind was believed to have driven the steamer off course. And now, in conditions of poor visibility, the second mate noticed a light ahead of the ship, although he had no idea what it was. Rather than taking immediate action to stop as would have been sensible, he called the captain up on deck instead, who, deciding that something was very wrong, promptly gave the order to put the engines into reverse at full power. Too late. A crashing sound was quickly followed by the ship hitting something very solid. The alarm was sounded and the crew readied themselves for an emergency. And now, even though the engines were running at full speed astern the ship would not budge.

Distress rockets were fired from the ship, and by the light of the glare, the *Chicago*'s predicament became clear – the ship was grounded on the rocks directly underneath Slains Castle. The light they had seen came from the castle's windows where a ball was underway in honour of the servants.

A coachman heard the distress rockets and contacted the coastguards, although by chance, one of them was on Cruden Bay beach and had seen the distress flares for himself. The two coastguards, Robert Sweetland and Reginald Lang, now fired the mortar to signal the village volunteers to bring up the life-saving apparatus.

On hearing the alarm in the castle, the ball came to a stop when everyone piled out on a wet, stormy night to watch the proceedings with great interest. The life-saving apparatus was brought up and a line fired by rocket draped across the stranded steamer on the second attempt. Within the hour, twenty-one men had been brought up one by one to the cliff top using a harness that could be hauled back and forth; the captain, first mate, and two engineers remaining on board to see what if anything could be done. They found three of the four ship compartments flooded and part of the engine room under water. The rocks that had cut open the starboard side of the ship during the collision were now what was pinning the ship in place.

When daylight came, it was confirmed that this was now a salvage operation. The *Chicago* had hit the cliff under Slains Castle with such an incredible force, large chunks of granite had sheared off in the collision, and a plank thrown loose by the collision had landed on the cliff top. Even when low tide came, the ship stayed put, the captain having hoped that the weight of the ship would make her slide off its cliff-side perch.

Over the next few days, the Port Erroll fishermen helped to salvage some of the freight including wine and tobacco. But this became too dangerous when the gradual shifting of the ship gave rise to the possibility that a sudden lurch could make it slip under water, trapping the men inside.

## 1895

**January:** Bram Stoker's short novel *The Watter's Mou'*, set in Port Erroll, was published by Constable and Co. on January 7, 1895. In a smuggling tale brought into the present day, the plot revolves around the agonising conflict of duty experienced by William Barrow, the coastguard, on discovering that his fiancée's father is due onshore with contraband brought over from Germany. It was the coastguard's responsibility to apprehend the boat as it came into the harbour, and, this being Victorian times, William considered himself beholden to his duty no matter what.

Maggie MacWhirter, William's fiancée, also appreciating this, courageously rows out from the Watter's Mou' (a sea gorge near Slains Castle) with a storm on the way. She contacts her father out to sea, and when she warns him he will be arrested on returning to the harbour, he throws the contraband overboard. When she returns to the coast, Maggie MacWhirter is drowned in the Watter's Mou', as is William Barrow when he tries to recover her body.

**March:** The efforts of the Port Erroll Dramatic Society have definitely not been appreciated according to a letter published in the *Buchan Observer* newspaper. On the first of the month they gave a performance of the play *East Lynne* in the village of Hatton, only for the audience to be vastly underwhelmed. The actors, we are informed, conducted the drama in a tame and schoolboy-like manner, thus failing to convey the full-bodied feeling the play deserved. The anonymous letter-writer added that to improve, the players must throw away that 'can't-we-do-it' attitude and engage in at least half the spirit of their roles before they could expect to be appreciated by a Hatton audience, or by any other intelligent audience for that matter.

A week later, the *Buchan Observer* published a reply from one of the actors, denouncing the ungentlemanly tone of the criticism, and accusing the letter-writer of disguising an attack on the people of Port Erroll as criticism of their performance. Such a bad review was undeserved, particularly as others had given unbounded praise to the amateur players in the group.

**April:** With the new railway under construction and plans for a new hotel and golf course, Port Erroll is now envisaged as the 'Brighton of the North'; in other words, an upmarket tourist resort. New plans for the expansion of the village have been revealed and sites for over 200 new houses identified. An accompanying map shows the lay-out of several crescents fronted by the new homes, together with a new public park and a cricket ground. The proposed railway station is shown at the south-east corner of the expanded village layout.

**June:** Excellent progress had been made on the new railway. Eight-hundred men were now working on the line, most of them from Glasgow or Ireland. Indeed, more men were required, and every navvy applying for work was immediately given a contract and put on the job. It had been a major undertaking to provide accommodation for all these men, a problem solved by building huts for them in the villages close to the railway. For example, the wooden huts in Port Erroll, which housed thirty men, were fitted out with bunk beds and a large table for meals and card-playing. They had everything they needed, 'intoxicating liquors excepted'.

The men were reasonably well behaved, although on pay night they invariably took off on a drinking spree, walking to any nearby town where alcohol was served, and then sleeping off the night by the roadside. Unimpressed by the men's drinking antics, the magistrates in Ellon increased the bails and fines for drunk and disorderly behaviour again and again on a weekly basis (probably to little effect).

The scale of the operation on the new railway hasbeen colossal: it involved four steam cranes, thirty hand cranes, four traction engines, and seventy horses. The granite used for bridges and viaducts was sourced from the Stirlinghill quarry near Peterhead and Kemnay quarry. Tractions engines brought the granite from nearby Stirlinghill, whereas the Kemnay granite was transported by train to Ellon, forty tons arriving every day.

Work on the line had now reached Port Erroll, where the biggest challenge of the entire operation will be to build a viaduct across the Cruden Water at Braehead, a farm next to the village. It will comprise three long iron girders supported by granite pillars - completion expected two months hence.

**July:** On the night of the 12$^{th}$ of this month, the gunboat *Jackal* caught the trawler *Lily* fishing inside the three-mile limit offshore from Port Erroll. The master of the trawler was later found guilty and fined at Aberdeen Sherrif Court.

**August:** Bram Stoker returned to Port Erroll for another month-long visit. Bram, Florence, and their son Noel separately signed the guest book at the Kilmarnock Arms Hotel. On this visit Bram will be writing the early chapters of his gothic horror novel *Dracula*.

Both Florence and Noel will become astonished by his behaviour that summer; Florence later telling a reporter they were all scared of him because 'he seemed to get obsessed by the spirit of the thing'. Bram spent hours sitting on the rocks of the shore 'like a giant bat' or striding up and down the beach thinking out what to write. Noel later told Bram's biographer that his father had been pushing ahead with his novel at full steam, and was 'very testy' that year.

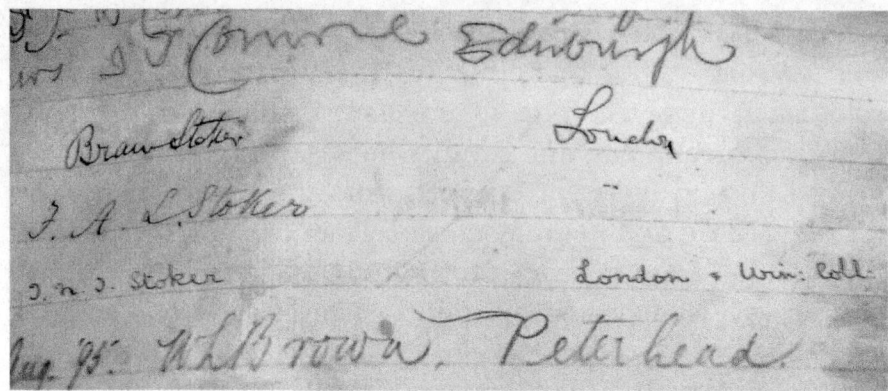

Bram Stoker's signature in the Kilmarnock Arms guest book for 1895.

Also this month, Adam Drummond resigned as the minister for Port Erroll Congregational Church. The exact reason why is unknown to us today. He had accepted a call to become minister for Macduff Congregational Church, and will take up his post there on August 18.

# 3. ADAM DRUMMOND'S STORIES AND ESSAYS.

The core of this book is provided by eleven short stories and sketches written by Reverend Adam Drummond, Minister of Port Erroll Congregational Church from 1891 to 1895. Using the Doric dialect, they tell of the day-to-day life and concerns of the fishing community of Port Erroll on the east coast of Aberdeenshire.

The short stories and sketches were never intended for publication: these are typewritten scripts for talks. Adam Drummond enjoyed public speaking at church meetings and to village societies on a variety of subjects. I have found one newspaper article that mentions him reciting his Port Erroll stories in a public meeting: the *Buchan Observer* newspaper reported on November 25, 1902, that some of the stories were read out to the Literary Society in the village of Hatton, and were 'rendered in the purest Doric of the East Coast'. They were evidently enjoyed by what was described as a full house.

The Doric dialect, also known as the Buchan dialect, is the variety of Scots spoken in rural North East Scotland. It is usually incomprehensible to outsiders, and I can share my personal experience of this. When I was six years old my father sold his public bar in Aberdeen and bought a farm near Turriff in rural Aberdeenshire. I now started school at Turriff Academy. Although my family had only moved thirty-four miles from Aberdeen, I discovered that on my first day at school I had no idea what anyone was saying to me - not a clue - it was as if I was experiencing a totally new language. I was now compelled to quickly understand and speak the Doric dialect should I wish to communicate with my new schoolmates. Although I do not speak Doric now, I understand it – hence my efforts at translating Adam Drummond's written Doric into English.

I must say that the Port Erroll Doric of the 1890s differs somewhat from the Doric I learnt in Turriff in the 1960s. Adam's dialogue contains more dialect words than are commonly used in modern Doric, and I also suspect that the spoken Doric of the fisher folk and farming folk differs somewhat, an observation confirmed to me by my neighbour Jill McWilliam in Cruden Bay. The English translations below have thus been augmented with help from the *Dictionary of the Scots Language*.

I'm told, even by native Doric speakers, that written Doric is difficult to read, and I reckon my translations will help the reader here. Even so, the Doric version as written by Adam Drummond is much more expressive by comparison to the English translation, possibly because English is too clunky a language for getting subtle nuances of feeling across unless you happen to be a brilliant writer or poet. All in all, I reckon that Adam Drummond's stories could readily end up being recognised as classics of Doric literature.

## HOW THE MESSAGE CAME (ORIGINAL)

There was sore trouble and much searching of heart in the Ward: such trouble as constantly lowers over a fisher community when sorrow is on the sea, and it cannot be quiet: such searching of heart as is common to all humanity, when the bread-winners are in peril and none can help. And to such peril had they come, for the wind blew from the north in awful gusts of terrific violence, tearing the frail roofs off exposed dwellings, scattering the sand hills over the village streets, and making strong men stagger in their steps. The brae face was studded with little scattered groups of men eagerly scanning with glasses each passing close-reefed sail as it scudded past, and ever and anon one could hear an eager word: 'Look here, that's a Ward boat!'

'Aye, that's Spunkie, see the white bit in her foresail.'

And then the glass would be shut with a clash, as the gazer turned away with a look of despair in his eyes, saying, 'Na, she's nae oors, she's frae Collieston.'

And the restless women, who fain would help husbands, brothers, and sons who had sailed forth in the early morning to fight their battles, haunted the hill top, with heads close swathed in shawls, in little despairing groups, uttering words of mutual sympathy that served only to dispel hope. Now and again one would leave a group, and, with skirts tossing in the blast, seek some solitary headland or isolated jutting rock, and gaze seaward, action, attitude, and set face all expressing one despairing thought, 'Wull ye no come back again?' And the women who could stay at home, having nerve to sit quiet, and look out dry clothes from chests and presses, said, 'I ken I couldna help them though I was wi' them, an' we're a' in gweed han's.'

There is real peril when the women speak in such fashion. The bay was quiet save for the bodeful cries of the sea-mews rising and falling or sliding sideways on the wind, and the snarling hiss of the long, black, sullen swell, rolling in from the outer seas, as it broke at length in curved rows of white cruel teeth on sand and shingle. But out at sea, when the waters meet the clouds, the jagged sky line, glittering white in dots and streaks, spoke to the experienced eye of wild work on the fishing grounds. The bay was sheltered by the headlands, but far out at sea the hurricane struck the fishing fleet as the boats lay by the lines. The fleet was scattered, each boat taking such course as necessity demanded, or skill decided.

A few reached the Ward, others found shelter in convenient ports, and others thought best to ride out the storm hanging on to floating anchors or 'drogs', hastily extemporised with booms and sails. It was a fearful time. The sea rose in huge green lumps of water covered with a lacework of white foam, which ever and anon broke with terrific force over the bows, dashing showers of spray over the main mast, and rushing like a millrace from stem to stern.

For three hours they hung on to the hawsers, the huge seas rushing alongside almost flush with the gunwale, and, with eyes blinded by driving spray, and half suffocated with a whirling drift of snow, the hardy fishers almost gave up hope. This was on Thursday, and on Saturday night, as darkness fell, two boats were amissing, and double darkness fell on the Ward.

On Sunday morning ere the sun had fully risen, the anxious watchers stood on the hilltop eagerly scanning the horizon for the wanderers. Hope was gone, but, as if kindred eyes might bring them, kindred eyes searched the gloom. At such moments of tension and despair we mutely acknowledge that God's first gift of life is the best. No gift would raise such joy in the Ward as the sight of two brown patched fishing sails. None such appeared that day, but a message came, and this is how it came.

Frazer had two sons in the *Bonnie Bess*. He went to bed

thinking he had two sons less in the world, and he rose on Sunday morning with a strange hope in his heart, saying to his wife, 'Betsy, I'm gyan to get a message the day.'

'Fu do ye ken that Frazer?' said his wife, looking up from the teapot she was filling for breakfast.

'Fu do I ken that!' he replied. 'Deed I dinna ken, but I jist ken - wait an' see.'

Frazer told me himself, so it is not a carried story. It may lose much in the retelling, for the spoken word is living, but you may trust on the truth of it.

'Weel ye see, it was this wye, Mr Duncan. On Setersday nicht we were a' gye sair made, as ye may ken, efter watchin a' day, an' nae news o' the boat. In the forenicht Babbie cam in - aye that's Oondy's Babbie ye ken, Geordie's sister, an' my ain gweedsister, weel she cam in an' newsed wi' the women folk afore we beddit. Gled I was to see her, fur a frien's face maks a lang nicht shortsome, an' we were a' gye sober kin' as we sat by the fire.

"Betsy," says she, "I'm sair dootin the news we may get the morn."

Wi' that Betsy hid her face in her han's, fur Babbie had houkit up a dreed she was tryin' tae hide frae hersel'. Than there was nae word spak for a lang while. The lasses sabbit quaet like, Betsy keepit her han's on her face, an' Babbie lookit vext.

Syne Babbie rase an' said, "Frazer, I maun awa' doon noo, but keep up yer hert, nae news is gweed news, they say, gweed nicht."

Syne we a' beddit, though there was little sleep for a curran o' us that nicht, but in the wink or twa I gat I had a dream. I dreamt I was stannin' afore my ain door, in the gloamin', newsin wi' Geordie, whan we baith heard a steamer's horn in the bay. She was jist comin' roon the Skares when we lookit, an' she steamed in an' anchored furnent the Salmon Hoose.

Geordie was jist sayin', "Fat can she be Frazer?" when she fired a shot oot o' her bows that cam scoorin up the road, roarin' like a rocket, an' leavin' a lang tail o' fiery sparks ahint it. It scuffed me an' Geordie as it derted bye, an' - be't we hadna joukit, it wad hae gruppet the baith o' us. It landed syne awa up the street, but naebody seemed to tak notice o't but me an' Geordie. Fan I lookit to my feet I saw something lyin' on the grun', an' I says, "Fat's that Geordie?"

Geordie looks an' says, "I kenna, but it looks like a wire carriet by the shot," but he never tried to grup it.

I lootit to tak haud, but try as I micht I ne'er could lay a finger on't: ye'l hae seen the like in dreams Mr Duncan? Ye'l try to shoot a gun, an' the trigger draws but the dougheid disna' fa', or, if the dougheid fa's, the powther disna catch, or if the powther catches, the chairge never gets far'er than the muzzle. Fat can that mean do ye think? Think ye we lauch at oorsel's in oor dreams, fur there's naething else in the warl' to lauch at, or think ye the dream is just the mind graipin' in the dark for the tail en' o' a thocht it has got the heid o' when we're waukin'. I've lang been bothered wi' ae thing in the Bible. Fat wye didna Balaam lauch whan the cuddie spak to him? Fyles I think he maun hae dreamt it, fur there's nae ferlies in my dreams.

But dootless Balaam was anither man frae me, at least I houp sae. Weel, as I was saying, I lootit, an' better lootit to grup that ware, but feint a ware could I grup, an' wi' that I waukened. Wad ye believe't! my first thocht was the boat. It cam duntin' up on my hert like a louse pulley block on the mainmast.

It was a new day, but an auld sair, an' the wecht o't was heavier that I kenned I had something to mind aboot. The women folk were up gettin' breakfast, an' I lay fechtin to grup what I had lost. A' at ance my dream cam back an' I kenned that was what I socht.

Said I to mysel! "Fat can it mean?"

"Frazer," says I, "It's a message, but fat is't aboot? It tells naething. A shot, a girnin' roar, a shoor o' fire, an' - than I mindit on the ware. That's it," says I, "it's a ware, that's what they ca' a telegraph."

Syne I could say at brakfast, "Betsy, I'm gyan to get a message the day, an' Betsy said, "Fu do ye ken that Frazer?"

It was ten minutes to aucht when I wan up to the Post Office, meanin' to sen' a message to Aiberdeen. The post wifie said to me, "Wait fur ten meenuts Frazer, an' than I'll see yer telegraph. There'l no be naebody at the tither en' yet."

Syne she sent my message speirin' news o' the boat, and than she said, "Wait for aucht meenuts an' ye'l get an' answer, sud ony ane be there."

Weel, I waitet aucht meenuts, ten meenuts, fifteen meenuts, twenty meenuts.

"I doot there's naebody there Frazer," says she, an' my hert sank, for I coontit on't. I had socht fur't an', as I thocht, got the promise o't. Syne whan I was thinkin' aboot gyan awa doon, maybe aboot twenty-wan, or maybe it might be twenty-twa meenuts efter aucht, an' the post-mistress was lookin' gye peetifu' at me, I heard a sherp and quick ting - ting.

"That's it noo," says she, an' ran to the telegraph boxie, rowin' roon yon wee han'lie, an' writin' letters oot as they cam'.

Says I, "Dinna write mistress, jist tell me the words as they come, I canna wait."

Weel, she gie me ae word, twa words, three words, me stannin' a' shakkin'.

"Thank God!" I says, "That's a' I want," and ran oot an' doon hame as fast's I could. But I didna get takin' my ain news, though I sud a likit sae weel, fur maist the hale toon was oot watchin' me, an' there Kirsty stood, half-rankit, at her ain door cryin', "What news, Frazer?"

"A's weel, Kirsty," says I, an' wi' that Kirsty ran, like a fule woman, half-rankit as she was, doon the toon cryin, "A's weel, a's weel." Wad ye believe't Mr. Duncan, the hale toon was oot, an' ilka ane mair gled than the ither, it lookit as if we had a' cam' into a lot o' siller. An' I hae thocht aboot it a gweed curran times sin syne an' said to mysel', "Fu was't naebody misdooted, my word? Fu was't they were a sae gled. an' sae ready tae be gled? There's oor minister, ilka Sabbath he tells the guid guid news to's, a' far better news than the comin' hame o' a boat, fur it's the makkin' o' a hame for the hale family o's an' they misdoot his word, an' few are made gled. Fu did they no' misdoot puir Frazer an' the truth o' his news?"

An' the only reddin' up o't is this, sae far's I can see, they were a hungerin' for gweed news, an' they a' wantit to believe me.'

The Salmon House and shed (the shed has since been demolished).

## HOW THE MESSAGE CAME (ENGLISH)

There was sore trouble and much searching of heart in the Ward: such trouble as constantly lowers over a fisher community when sorrow is on the sea, and it cannot be quiet: such searching of heart as is common to all humanity, when the bread-winners are in peril and none can help. And to such peril had they come, for the wind blew from the north in awful gusts of terrific violence, tearing the frail roofs off exposed dwellings, scattering the sand hills over the village streets, and making strong men stagger in their steps. The hill face was studded with little scattered groups of men eagerly scanning with telescopes each passing close-reefed sail as it scudded past, and ever and anon one could hear an eager word: 'Look here, that's a Ward boat!'

'Aye, that's Spunkie, see the white bit in her foresail.'

And then the telescope would be shut with a clash, as the gazer turned away with a look of despair in his eyes, saying, 'No, she's not ours, she's from Collieston.'

And the restless women, who happily would help husbands, brothers, and sons who had sailed forth in the early morning to fight their battles, haunted the hill top, with heads close-swathed in shawls, in little despairing groups, uttering words of mutual sympathy that served only to dispel hope. Now and again one would leave a group, and, with skirts tossing in the blast, seek some solitary headland or isolated jutting rock, and gaze seaward, action, attitude, and set face all expressing one despairing thought, 'Will you not come back again?'

And the women who could stay at home, having nerve to sit quiet, and look out dry clothes from chests and presses, said, 'I know I couldn't help them even though I was with them, and we are all in good hands.'

There is real peril when the women speak in such fashion. The bay was quiet save for the baleful cries of the seagulls rising and falling or sliding sideways on the wind, and the snarling hiss of the long, black, sullen swell, rolling in from the outer seas, as it broke at length in curved rows of white cruel teeth on sand and shingle. But out at sea, where the waters meet the clouds, the jagged sky line, glittering white in dots and streaks, spoke to the experienced eye of wild work on the fishing grounds. The bay was sheltered by the headlands, but far out at sea the hurricane struck the fishing fleet as the boats lay by the lines. The fleet was scattered, each boat taking such course as necessity demanded, or skill decided.

A few reached the Ward, others found shelter in convenient ports, and others thought best to ride out the storm hanging on to floating anchors or sea anchors, hastily extemporised with booms and sails. It was a fearful time. The sea rose in huge green lumps of water covered with a lacework of white foam, which ever and anon broke with terrific force over the bows, dashing showers of spray over the main mast, and rushing like a millrace from stem to stern.

For three hours they hung on to the hawsers, the huge seas rushing alongside almost flush with the gunwale, and, with eyes blinded by driving spray, and half suffocated with a whirling drift of snow, the hardy fishers almost gave up hope. This was on Thursday, and on Saturday night, as darkness fell, two boats were missing, and double darkness fell on the Ward.

On Sunday morning ere the sun had fully risen, the anxious watchers stood on the hilltop eagerly scanning the horizon for the wanderers. Hope was gone, but, as if kindred eyes might bring them, kindred eyes searched the gloom. At such moments of tension and despair we mutely acknowledge that God's first gift of life is the best. No gift would raise such joy in the Ward as the sight of two brown patched fishing sails. None such appeared that day, but a message came, and this is how it came.

Frazer had two sons in the *Bonnie Bess*. He went to bed thinking he had two sons less in the world, and he rose on

Sunday morning with a strange hope in his heart, saying to his wife, 'Betsy, I'm going to get a message today.'

'How do you know that Frazer?' said his wife, looking up from the teapot she was filling for breakfast.

'How do I know that!' he replied, 'Indeed I don't know but I just know - wait and see.'

Frazer told me himself, so it is not a carried story. It may lose much in the retelling, for the spoken word is living, but you may trust on the truth of it.

'Well you see, it was this way, Mr Duncan. On Saturday night we were all very upset, as you may know, after watching all day, and with no news of the boat. In the evening Babbie came in - aye that's Oondy's Babbie you know, Geordie's sister, and my sister-in-law, well she came in and gossiped with the women folk before we went to bed. Glad I was to see her, because a friendly face makes a long night short, and we were all pretty solemn as we sat by the fire.

"Betsy," says she, "I'm very doubtful about the news that we may get tomorrow."

With that Betsy hid her face in her hands, because Babbie had hooked up a dread she was trying to hide from herself. Then there was no word spoken for a long while. The lasses sobbed quietly, Betsy kept her hands on her face, and Babbie looked vexed.

Then Babbie rose and said, "Frazer, I must leave, but keep up your hearts, no news is good news, they say, good night."

Then we went to bed, although there was little sleep for some of us that night, but in a wink or two I had a dream. I dreamt I was standing in front of my door at sundown, gossiping with Geordie, when we both heard a steamer's horn in the bay. She was just coming round the Skares [the reefs extending half a mile out to sea near the southern end of the Bay of Cruden] when we looked, and she steamed in and anchored in front of the Salmon House. Geordie was just saying, "What can she be Frazer?" when she fired a shot out of her bows that came speeding up the road, roaring like a rocket, and leaving a long tail of fiery sparks behind it. It scuffed me and Geordie as it darted by, and if we hadn't ducked it would have hit both of us. It landed some way up the street, but nobody seemed to take notice of it but me and Geordie. When I looked to my feet I saw something lying on the ground, and I said, "What's that Geordie?"

Geordie looks and says, "I don't know but it looks like a wire carried by the shot," but he never tried to grasp it.

I stooped down to take hold, but try as I might I never could lay a finger on it: you will have seen the like in dreams Mr Duncan? You try to shoot a gun, and the trigger draws but the hammer doesn't fall, or, if the hammer falls, the powder doesn't go off, or if the powder catches, the charge never gets further than the muzzle. What can that mean do you think? We laugh at ourselves in our dreams, because there's nothing else in the world to laugh at, or you think the dream is just the mind groping in the dark for the tail end of a thought it heeds when we're waking. I've long been bothered with one thing in the Bible. Why didn't Balaam laugh when the ass spoke to him? While I think he may have dreamed it, there are no strange and wonderful thoughts in my dreams.

But doubtless Balaam was different from me at least I hope so. Well, as I was saying, I stooped down to grip the wire, but what the Devil if there was a wire there I could grip, and with that I wakened. Would you believe it my first thought was the boat. It came thumping up on my heart like a loose pulley block on the mainmast.

It was a new day, but an old sore, and the weight of it was heavier because I knew I had something to think about. The women folk were up getting breakfast, and I lay fighting to grasp what I had lost. All at once my dream came back and I knew what it was I sought.

Said I to myself! "What can it mean?"

"Frazer," says I, "It's a message, but what is it about? It tells nothing. A shot, a crying roar, a shower of fire, and then I remembered the wire. That's it," says I, "it's a wire, that's what they call a telegraph."

I said at breakfast, "Betsy, I'm going to get a message the day", and Betsy said, "How do you know that Frazer?"

It was ten minutes to eight when I went up to the Post Office, intending to send a message to Aberdeen. The post mistress said to me, "Wait for ten minutes Frazer, and then I'll see your telegraph. There will be nobody at the other end yet." She sent my message asking for news of the boat, and then she said, "Wait for eight minutes and you will get an answer should anyone be there."

Well, I waited eight minutes, ten minutes, fifteen minutes, twenty minutes.

"I doubt there's anybody there Frazer," says she, and my heart sank, for I had counted on it. I had sought it, and as I thought, had got the promise of it. Then when I was thinking about leaving, maybe about twenty-one or maybe it might have been twenty-two minutes after eight, and the post-mistress was looking with great pity at me, I heard a sharp and quick ting - ting.

"That's it now," says she, and ran to the telegraph box, turning round the wee handle and writing letters out as they came.

Says I, "Don't write mistress, just tell me the words as they come, I can't wait."

Well, she gave me one word, two words, three words, me standing and shaking.

"Thank God!" I says, "That's all I want," and ran out and went back home as fast as I could. But I didn't get to take my news, though I should have liked very much to do so, because most of the town was out watching me, and there Kirsty stood, half-wild, at her door crying "What news, Frazer?"

"All's well, Kirsty," says I, and with that Kirsty ran like a mad woman, half-wild she was, running down the town crying, "All's well, all's well."

Would you believe it Mr. Duncan, the whole town was out, and no man happier than the other, it looked as if we had all come into a great deal of money. And I have thought about it a good many times since then and said to myself, "How was it nobody misdoubted, my word? How was it they were all so glad, and so ready to be glad? There's our minister, every Sabbath he tells the good news to us and far better news than the coming home of a boat, because it's the making of a home for the whole family of us. Misdoubt his word, and few are made glad. How did they not misdoubt the truth of my news?"

And the only summing up of it is this: as far as I can see, they were all hungering for good news, and they all wanted to believe me.'

Port Erroll Post Office.

## WHY PEGSIE'S BLIND WAS NOT DRAWN (ORIGINAL)

The sun glinted through the rifts of scudding clouds, and the bent bowed and shivered before a cold blast from the sea as Frazer opened his door and stepped into the village street on the Monday morning after his message came. He looked at the sky and the sea, and an expression of deep content overspread his bronzed face, and softened the hard lines about his mouth. The sky was rakish looking, and the sea, rolling in big waves past the harbour mouth, and roaring on the beach, seemed to shout, 'No fishing today.' Frazer was glad, for the excitement of yesterday was still agitating him like a ground swell after a storm, and a day's 'newsin'' with hands in his trouser pockets would let him gently down from his height of excitement and distinction.

One figure stood in the lea of 'The Merchant's' house lighting his morning pipe. It was Jimsie, and Frazer approached him, got his back square up to the wall, and said, 'A roch mornin' Jimsie, hoo's the gless?'

'Oh she's doon again,' said Jimsie, pulling at his pipe.

'Could ye len' us a preen man? she's no sookin' richt.'

'A' things gang conter this w'ather.'

'Fu that?' said Frazer.

'Oh a' wyes',' replied Jimsie.

'Man I was to gang to the kirk yesterday, an' was thinkin' lang to gang, but it was half eleven afore I waukent, an' the wife said I didna tell her. Fine she kens I wis to gang.'

'I wunner if Paul was mairrit, Frazer.'

'Fu' man?' cried Frazer, 'yer dottlet. Fat has Paul to dae wi' you an yer sleepy heid?'

Jimsie lazily turned his other shoulder to the wall and said: 'I'm thinkin' Frazer that Paul had a curran tribbles he keeps his thoom on. Disna he say, "The things he wantit to dae, fouk keepit him frae daein', and the things he didna want to dae they garr'd him dae?" Noo, fa' in a' the warl could dae sic like wi' Paul 'cep it was his ain wife?'

Jimsie was a deep man, though you would not have thought so to see his round, red, good-humoured face, fringed with a tangled thicket of reddish grey whiskers, his fat well-to-do body rotund and comfortable, or his variegated ill-to-do trousers bulging much at the knees with frequent sitting. But a keen observer would see a gleam of humour in his small grey eye, and a lurking sense of his own importance in the style he showed when stopping his pipe with the point of his little finger.

Jimsie was not a successful fisherman. If two boats failed, his was sure to be one of them. His favourite text was 'Many are the tribulations of the righteous'. But he never failed to rear as many potatoes in his little plot among the sand hills as kept the 'loonies' eating all the winter, and he made the most of his success. He was conscious of a new distinction today, for he alone of all the men knew why Pegsie's blind was not drawn. One other house the secret was known, but they had promised not to 'news' about it. For the last twenty-four hours this was the subject that had exercised the keenest intellects of the Ward.

Yesterday, when Kirsty ran down the village street shouting Frazer's message from the sea, 'A's weel! - A's weel!', every blind was drawn but one, every door was opened but one, every household was represented on the village street but one, and that one was Jimsie's Pegsie's.

A little thing gives a man distinction in the Ward. If a boy showed good powers in mastering the intricacies of the rule of three at school, he might rest on his laurels as a 'keen loonie', 'a gran' scholar'. A strange disease, baffling the skill of all doctors and succumbing only before the power of a mysterious 'Yerb' called 'he-broom', would set a man up for life. The disease might become mythical, and be known darkly as 'Anomia on the stomach', but the man himself was continuously referred to as a distinguished example of Ward originality. One supreme moment of exciting life endows a man with a secret.

Frazer was king yesterday; Jimsie is king today, for a little thing might shunt a man off into a siding to make room for the new comer.

Jimsie's remarks about Paul were only intended to put Frazer off the scent, and as, by this time, several fishermen had gathered in the lea of the merchant's house, he continued his moralising to a larger audience.

'Ye can say fat ye like, Frazer, but things a' gang conter ee'noo. The lastest time the Captain gaed oot in Duthie's boat to fish, feint a fish gat he, though Duthie had a curran saft partans fur bait. Fan they cam' in the Captain says he, speaking Buchan kin', says he: "Duthie, it's nae eese."

"Fat fur no?" says Duthie speakin' as braid's he could. An' the Captain didna tak' up the words nae mair than the haddies. Noo, if that's no conter, I kenna fat's conter, fur the Captain's a keen ane.'

Here Oondy broke in saying, 'But Jimsie, no to interrup' ye, micht I be alloed to pit a quastion to ye?'

'Speer awa,' cried Jimsie.

'If things be a' sae conter as ye say, fat's the rizzon o' the conterness ee'noo?'

'It's the meen,' replied Jimsie with a cunning look. 'She's clean oot o' her coorse for the time o' year. 1 lookit her last nicht at twal' an' the tae half o' her glintet owre Hawklaw, fan she sud a been hyne awa' up ten or a dizzen yairds in the heevens. The meen rules the tides, as ye a' sud ken, an' naebody can tell fu' muckle mair she rules. But there's something wrang wi' her. A was newsin' wi' a man on Fairsday last, an' he telt me he had it frae his ain kizzen fa saw't in a Lunnon paper, that there was a great collusion in the meen, an' I'm dootin' she's been cantit on her beam, an' dung oot o' her coorse.'

'Root awa!' cried Oondy laughing, 'Yer cantit yersel'. Was't the meen that jam't yer window blind yesterday? Ye couldna win bye ohn hearin' Kirsty tearin' doon the street wi' Frazer's telegraph.'

This was too straight a thrust to be parried, and Jimsie, taking his pipe from his mouth, and wiping his mouth with the back of his hand, replied, as he lounged off, 'Speer that at Pegsie. I ken nocht aboot window blinds. Sud ye want news o' the meen I'm ready for ye.'

A loud laugh greeted this sally, but Oondy stood meditating.

At last he said: 'I kenna fat can be the rizzon o' that blind. Jimsie cam' hame on Setersday nicht gey sair made aboot Sandie. His boat wasna accoontit fur ye ken, an' Jimsie an' Pegsie wur jist as keen on news as ony o's. Aither he didna ken, or he didna care, or he didna want to hear gweed news till he got it o's ain. If he didna ken, they maun a' hae been sleepin', fur Kirsty micht a roosed the Castle folk, an' that's no like Jimsie or Pegsie, fur the thocht o' Sandie wad keepit them waukin'. If he wasna carin', it's far on-liker Jimsie, fur Jimsie's a naetral hertet man, an' if he had nae pleesure in Frazer's news, than I gi'e him up.'

'But they wur sleepin',' broke in Frazer. 'Jimsie telt me it was half eleven afore they waukent.'

'Na! Na! They war nae a' sleepin',' cried Stumpie, a short thick-set man, whose emphatic way of setting down his feet had gained him his tee name. 'They wur nae a' sleepin', for Sandy's Nancy saw a finger turnin' the edge o' the blind fan Kirsty ran bye, an' Pegsie keekit oot.'

'Weel that beats a'!' cried Oondy. 'I canna see the boddam o' this, but if it has a boddam I'll win to't.' After a few moments silent meditation, during which Oondy's eyebrows met together above his nose he said, 'Was Pegsie sair made kin' fan she keekit oot?'

'Fegs na,' said Stumpie, 'Sandy's Nancy says she was lauchin' kin'.' Oondy slapped his thigh and said: 'Div ony o' you chaps ken if Sandy cam' back late on Setersday or sune on Sabbath?'

'Aye did he,' cried out a woman from a doorway on the other side of the narrow street: 'Jimsie chappit us up at half-ane on

Sabbath mornin' to tell's that Sandy was hame. But keep's a', fat am I daein'? I wasna to tell naebody.'

The woman vanished in confusion within the doorway, followed by the laughter of the fishermen, and Oondy said: 'A weel, it's Sandy that's at the boddom o't, an' it micht hae a waur boddom than Sandy, peer chap, but I maun hae a haud wi' Jimsie aboot this yet.'

While the Ward in all its parts was exercised by this weighty question, the minister got the whole story from Pegsie in a moment of confidence.

'Come awa in an' sit doon,' said Pegsie, as the minister appeared in the doorway. 'Tak' a sate,' she continued, as she wiped a chair with a damp cloth to ensure a comfortable seat. 'I was thinkin' lang to see ye Mr. Duncan, an' I thocht it gey queer to see ye gaun bye my door on Setersday. I saw ye gaun in to Murdy's an' Soey's, an' I widna fin' faut for ye daein' sic like, for it was jist fat ye sud a done, but I was sair ta'en fan ye gaed bye ma door an' me a' my lane. Says I to mysel', 'Naebody thinks o' me an' my sorra, but weel wyte the Lord hisna forgotten me.'

'But,' said the minister, rather taken aback by this salutation, 'I did not know that you had been in trouble Mrs. Ray. As soon as I was aware of the anxiety about the two boats I went to see those who were most concerned.'

'Aye,' said she, 'that's jist fat I said. 'Ye didna ken or ye wad hae come to see me, but that maks the thing a' the waur, fur if fouk had mindit me they wad ha' telt ye: but a' body thinks aboot themsel's; a hantle fouk are convertet, but no mony naitrel hertet. Forgi'e me, Sir, but peer fouk hae their feelin's tae.'

'What then was your trouble Mrs. Ray?' said the minister. 'I did not know your husband had been at sea.'

'Weel ye see, Sir, it was this wye. It was the twa Ward boats the fouk were a thinkin' aboot, an' quite naitral, but oor Sandy, peer loonie, was in a Petershead boat, an' fan Setersday mornin' cam' an' nae word o' her, Jimsie wasna to haud, but maun be aff wi' the bus to see fu' if there was nae word ava. He hung aboot the herbour a' day, an' twa or three boats cam' in, but nane had seen oor Sandy's. Well, he waited till sax o'clock, an' than he cam' awa hame, trampin' a the road wi' a sair hert, for he couldna' think there was ony hope. Fan I sees Jimsie comin' doon the toon a' by himsel' my hert near stoppit for I saw by his face he had nae gweed news.

It was a sair nicht fur the baith o's, fur the loss o' a son's a sair nip, an', forbye, though Sandy's a gweed kin' loonie, he's no' convertit yet ye ken, an' sae we had nae sure hope to lichten oor sorra. We gat the little'ns beddit, an' syne we beddit oorsel's, but nane o's gat nae sleep that nicht. Fan I heard the loonie an' the quynie drawin' lang sechs in their soon' sleep I wished I was a bairn jist to sleep an' forget Sandy. Than I thocht I wad raither be Sandy's Mither an' greet for him, lyin' cauld, wi' the tangle wavin' owre's heid.

Better to be Sandy's Mither an' greet for him, than no to be his Mither an' lauch, for Sandy's a gweed loonie, an' a kin' ane. Weel I lay thinkin' an' I thocht Jimsie was sleepin', an' a thocht it was selfish kin' o'm to leave me to bear my sorra a' my lane, but I vrang't Jimsie, fur peer man he had his ain tribbles. He was Sandy's faither if I was his mither, an' ane sudna forget his neebor's sair heid tho' his ain teeth's goupin'.

I sudna maybe say this to ye Sir, but I ken ye'l no be newsin' aboot it, an' it helps a woman body to tell things. Me an' Jimsie had a word on Friday's nicht: ye ken Jimsie's a thocht quick kin', tho' he's a gweed man to me. Weel, at antern times we hae a bit word like that, an' than he'l no speak muckle for a day or twa, an' I never say naething aither 'cep fan we're at oor meat, fan I'll say, "Mak a piece for yersel' man, yer at yer ain firen'".

Than he'll jist begin naitrel kin' fan we're reddin the lines, an' oor fingers meet at a hard tangle, an' than the thing blaws bye withoot a word aboot it. But sorra that belangs to twa fouk brings they fouk thegither. As I was sayin', I thocht he was sleepin', an' a gied a sech, an' fat sud Jimsie dae but pat his tae han' on mine, sic like as he did fan we was lad an' lass an' said: "I was owre quick wi' ye Pegsie lass: I'm thinkin' lang for Sandy."

"Na Jimsie," says I, "it was me an' no you," an' my hert was lichter kin', for if I had lost Sandy I had gotten my ain man. Weel, jist wi' that I heard through the sough o' the win' a chap at the window. It wad be aboot half-ane, an' I was eerie kin' thinkin' o' the chaps that come to some fouks at siccan times fan their ain fouk are droonin'.

I was lyin' shakkin', an' Jimsie speert at me fat was vrang wi' me, fan anither chap cam to the window, an' neist a word "Mither! Mither!".

"That's Sandy" says I, an' throwin' aff the claes I was at the door afore Jimsie kent fat was adae. I didna say "Fa's there?" I jist flang open the door an' syne cried "Is that you?", an' Sandy's voice said, "Aye it's me Mither, lat me in oot o' the weet." I wat I was na lang or I lat him in, an' then he stood wi' the watter rinnin' aff him in dubs on the flare.

Jimsie was like a feel man; he sprang frae's bed an' gruppit Sandy by's baith han's. He never spak, but drew on his breeks and ran oot in the rain to chap up Nancy's fouk. An' naething wad dae but they maun come in to see oor Sandy, sae muckle is he respeckit. Ane never kens hoo muckle they're respeckit till ane comes back frae the deid. I gat dry claes for him an' kennl't the fire, an' pat on the teapot, an' I was to pit a speldin' on the brander, but afore I kent fat I was doin' I pat a saft biscuit on instead o' the speldin'. Sandy leuch, an' syne fan a' was ready we had a gran' cozy supper amang oorsel's.

Syne Sandy and Jimsie lichtit their pipes, an' Sandy telt us a' aboot it. His boat cam in through the win' an' rain, an' fan he steppit ashore at Petersheid, Rabsie Forbes telt him that his faither had been seekin' him a' day. He was jist drookit wi' saut watter for the seas wer washin' owre them fur 'oors, but fan he heard fu' that me an' Jimsie were sae sair made aboot him he set aff frae Petersheid an' trampit through the rain to set oor minds at rest. It's a gweed aucht miles frae Petersheid, maister Duncan, an' I think that's ae' pint that'l stan' on Sandy's side fan a's coontit. Weel, fan a' was telt, we beddit again, an', as ye ken, nane o's got to the Kirk, for we were a' wearit oot for want of sleep.

Fan Kirsty ran doon wi' Frazer's telegraph I keekit bye the

blind, but didna draw't up. The fouk wunnert aboot it, an' I hear they were quarrellin' us for want o' kin'ly feelin. But ye see, oor ain was come hame, an' that was the wye the blind wasna drawn.

An' yer gaun awa Maister Duncan; thenk ye kin'ly for comin', an' haste ye back.'

A fisher wife and her collection of baskets, Port Erroll.

## WHY PEGSIE'S BLIND WAS NOT DRAWN (ENGLISH)

The sun glinted through the rifts of scudding clouds, and the bent bowed and shivered before a cold blast from the sea as Frazer opened his door and stepped into the village street on the Monday morning after his message came. He looked at the sky and the sea, and an expression of deep content spread over his bronzed face, and softened the hard lines about his mouth. The sky was rakish looking, and the sea, rolling in big waves past the harbour mouth, and roaring on the beach, seemed to shout, 'No fishing today'. Frazer was glad, for the excitement of yesterday was still agitating him like a ground swell after a storm, and a day's gossiping with hands in his trouser pockets would let him gently down from his height of excitement and distinction.

One figure stood in the lea of the merchant's house lighting his morning pipe. It was Jimsie, and Frazer approached him, got his back square up to the wall, and said, 'A rough morning Jimsie, how's the barometer?'

'Oh she's down again,' said Jimsie, pulling at his pipe.

'Could you lend me a pin, man? My pipe's not sucking right.'

'Everything's going contrary in this weather.'

'How's that?' said Frazer.

'Oh always,' replied Jimsie.

'I was going to go to the church yesterday, and I was thinking long to go, but it was half eleven before I woke up and the wife said I didn't tell her. She knew only too well that I was intending to go.'

'I wonder if Saint Paul was married, Frazer.'

'Who man?' cried Frazer, 'you are befuddled. What has Paul to do with you and your sleepy head?'

Jimsie lazily turned his other shoulder to the wall and said:

'I'm thinking Frazer that Paul had a small number of troubles he kept his thumb on. Didn't he say "the things he wanted to do, folk kept him from doing them, and the things he didn't want to do they made him do?" Now, who in all the world could do this with Paul except it was his own wife?'

Jimsie was a deep man, though you would not have thought so to see his round, red, good-humoured face, fringed with a tangled thicket of reddish grey whiskers, his fat well-to-do body, rotund and comfortable, or his variegated ill-to-do trousers bulging much at the knees with frequent sitting. But a keen observer would see a gleam of humour in his small grey eye, and a lurking sense of his own importance in the style he showed when stopping his pipe with the point of his little finger.

Jimsie was not a successful fisherman. If two boats failed, his was sure to be one of them. His favourite text was 'many are the tribulations of the righteous'. But he never failed to rear as many potatoes in his little plot among the sand hills as kept the boys eating all winter, and he made the most of his success. He was conscious of a new distinction today, for he alone of all the men knew why Pegsie's blind was not drawn. In one other house the secret was known, but they had promised not to 'news' about it. For the last twenty-four hours this was the subject that had exercised the keenest intellects of the Ward.

Yesterday, when Kirsty ran down the village street shouting Frazer's message, 'All's well! - All's well!', every blind was drawn but one, every door was opened but one, every household was represented on the village street but one, and that one was Jimsie's Pegsie's.

A little thing gives a man distinction in the Ward. If a boy showed good powers in mastering the intricacies of the rule of three at school, he might rest on his laurels as a 'keen boy', 'a grand scholar'. A strange disease, baffling the skill of all doctors and succumbing only before the power of a mysterious 'herb' called 'he-broom' [Laburnum], would set a man up for life. The disease might become mythical and be known darkly as 'Anomia on the stomach', but the man himself was continuously referred to as a distinguished example of Ward originality. One supreme moment of exciting life endows a man with a secret.

Frazer was king yesterday; Jimsie is king today, for a little thing might shunt a man off into a siding to make room for the new comer.

Jimsie's remarks about Paul were only intended to put Frazer off the scent, and as, by this time, several fishermen had gathered at the side of the merchant's house, he continued his moralising to a larger audience.

'You can say what you like, Frazer, but things are contrary at the moment. The last time the Captain went out in Duthie's boat to fish, not a fish he got, though Duthie had a small number of soft crabs for bait. When they came in the Captain says he, speaking in the Buchan dialect: "Duthie, it's no use." "What's up now?" says Duthie speaking as broad as he could. And the Captain didn't take up the words any more than the haddocks. Now, if that's not contrary, I don't know what is, because the Captain's a perceptive one.'

Here Oondy broke in saying, 'But Jimsie, not to interrupt you, might I be allowed to put a question to you?'

'Fire away,' cried Jimsie.

'If things be all so contrary as you say, what's the reason for it just now?'

'It's the moon,' replied Jimsie with a cunning look. 'She's clean out of her course for the time of year. 1 looked at her last night at twelve, and the toe of the half moon was glinting over Hawklaw, when she should have been higher up by up ten or a dozen yards in the heavens. The moon rules the tides, as you all should know, and nobody can tell how much more she rules. But there's something wrong with her. I was chatting to a man on Thursday last, and he told me he had been told by his cousin who saw it in a London paper that there was a great collision in the moon, and I believe she has been rolled over on her beam and knocked out of her course.'

'Get away with you!' cried Oondy laughing, 'You are knocked out of true yourself. Was it the moon that jammed your window blind yesterday? You must have heard Kirsty tearing down the street with Frazer's telegraph.'

This was too straight a thrust to be parried, and Jimsie, taking his pipe from his mouth, and wiping his mouth with the back of his hand, replied, as he lounged off, 'Ask Pegsie. I know nothing about window blinds. Should you want news of the moon I'm ready for you.'

A loud laugh greeted this sally, but Oondy stood thinking.

At last he said: 'I don't know why the blind was drawn. Jimsie came home on Saturday night upset about Sandie. His boat wasn't accounted for you know, and Jimsie and Pegsie were just as keen on news as any of us. Either he did not know, or he didn't care, or he didn't want to hear good news until he got it of his own. If he didn't know, they must all have been sleeping, because Kirsty might have roused the Castle folk, and that's not like Jimsie or Pegsie, because the thought of Sandie would have kept them awake. If he wasn't caring, it's not like Jimsie, because Jimsie's a naturally-hearted man, and if he had no pleasure in Frazer's news, then I would give up on him.'

'But they were sleeping,' broke in Frazer. 'Jimsie told me it was half eleven before they were awake.'

'No! No! They were not sleeping,' cried Stumpie, a short thick-set man, whose emphatic way of setting down his feet had gained him his tee name. 'They were not sleeping, because Sandy's Nancy saw a finger turning the edge of the blind when Kirsty ran by, and Pegsie peered out.'

'Well that beats all!' cried Oondy. 'I cannot see the bottom of this, but if it has a bottom I'll find it.' After a few moments silent meditation, during which Oondy's eyebrows met together above his nose he said, 'Was Pegsie upset when she looked out?'

'Faith no,' said Stumpie. 'Sandy's Nancy says she was laughing.'

Oondy slapped his thigh and said: 'Do any of you chaps know if Sandy came back late on Saturday or early on Sunday?'

'Aye, he did,' cried out a woman from a doorway on the other side of the narrow street: 'Jimsie knocked on our door at half-one on Sunday morning to tell us that Sandy was home. But what am I doing? I was not to tell anybody.'

The woman vanished in confusion within the doorway, followed by the laughter of the fishermen, and Oondy said: 'Ah well, it's Sandy that's at the bottom of it, and there might be something bad here, poor chap, but I must talk with Jimsie about this even so.'

While the Ward in all its parts was exercised by this weighty question, the minister got the whole story from Pegsie in a moment of confidence.

'Come away in and sit down,' said Pegsie, as the minister appeared in the doorway. 'Take a seat,' she continued, as she wiped a chair with a damp cloth to ensure a comfortable seat. 'I was thinking long to see you Mr Duncan, and I thought it rather strange to see you going past my door on Saturday. I saw you going in to Murdy's and Soey's, and I wouldn't find fault for you doing this, for it was just what you should have done, but I was taken back when you went past my door. Says I to myself, 'Nobody thinks of me and my sorrow, but God hasn't forgotten me.'

'But,' said the Minister, rather taken aback by this salutation, 'I did not know that you had been in trouble Mrs. Ray. As soon as I was aware of the anxiety about the two boats I went to see those who were most concerned.'

'Aye,' said she, 'That's just what I said. You didn't know or you would have come to see me, but that makes the thing all the worse, because if folk had thought of me they would have told you: but everybody thinks about themselves; many people are converted, but not many are naturally hearted. Forgive me, Sir, but poor folk have their feelings too.'

'What then was your trouble Mrs. Ray?' said the minister, 'I did not know your husband had been at sea.'

'Well you see, Sir, it was this way. It was the two Ward boats the folk were all thinking about, and quite naturally, but our Sandy, poor boy, was in a Peterhead boat, and when Saturday morning came and there was no word of her, Jimsie wasn't going to hang around, but went off with the bus to see why nothing had been heard. He hung about the harbour all day, and two or three boats came in, but none had seen our Sandy's. Well, he waited till six o'clock, and then he came home, tramping along the road with a sore heart, for he didn't believe there was any hope. When I saw Jimsie coming down the town all by himself my heart near stopped for I saw by his face he had no good news.

It was a sore night for the both of us, because the loss of a son is a sore bite, and although Sandy's a good kind boy, he's not converted yet you know, and so we had no sure hope to lighten our sorrow. We got the little ones to bed, and then we went to bed ourselves, but neither of us got any sleep that night. When I heard the boy and the girl drawing long sighs in their deep sleep I wished I was a child just to sleep and forget Sandy. Then I thought I would rather be Sandy's mother and cry for him, lying cold, with the seaweed waving over his head.

Better to be Sandy's mother and cry for him, than not to be his mother, for Sandy's a good boy, and a kind one. Well I lay thinking and I thought Jimsie was sleeping, and I thought it was selfish of him to leave me to bear my sorrow on my own, but I wronged Jimsie, because poor man he had his own troubles. He was Sandy's father if I was his mother, and one shouldn't forget his neighbour's grief even though his own teeth is grinding.

I should not maybe say this to you sir, but I know you will not be gossiping about it, and it helps a woman to tell things. Me and Jimsie had an argument on Friday night: you know Jimsie's thought to be quick-tempered, though he's a good man to me. Well, at odd moments we argue, and then he will not speak much for a day or two, and I never say anything either except when we are having a meal.

Then he'll just begin naturally, just like when we are untangling and cleaning the fishing lines together, and our fingers meet at a hard tangle, and then thing blows by without a word about it. But sorrow that belongs to two people brings those people together. As I was saying, I thought he was sleeping, and I gave a sigh, and what should Jimsie do but put his two hands on mine, just as he did when we were lad and lass, and said: "I was over quick with you Pegsie lass, I keep thinking about Sandy."

"No Jimsie," says I, "It was me and not you." And my heart was lighter, for if I had lost Sandy I had gotten my own man. Well, just with that I heard through the cry of the wind a knock at the window. It would be about half-one, and I was eerily thinking of the knocks that come to some people at the moment when their own folk are drowning.

I was lying shaking, and Jimsie guessed what was wrong with me, when another knock came to the window, and next came a word, "Mother! Mother!".

"That's Sandy," says I, and throwing off the blankets I was at the door before Jimsie knew what was ado. I didn't say "Who's there?" I just flung open the door and then cried, "Is that you?", and Sandy's voice said, "Aye it's me mother, let me in out of the wet." I let him in, and then he stood with the water running off him and forming black pools on the floor.

Jimsie was like a mad man; he sprang from his bed and gripped Sandy by both of his hands. He never spoke, but drew on his trousers and ran out in the rain to knock on the doors of Nancy's folk. And nothing would do but they must come in to see our Sandy, so much is he respected. One never knows how much they're respected till one comes back from the dead. I got dry clothes for him and lit the fire, and put on the teapot, and I was to put a dried herring on the grill, but before I knew what I was doing I put a soft biscuit on instead of the herring. Sandy laughed, and then when I was ready we had a grand cosy supper among ourselves.

Then Sandy and Jimsie lit their pipes, and Sandy told us all about it. His boat came in through the wind and rain, and when he stepped ashore at Peterhead, Rabsie Forbes told him that his father had been looking for him all day. He was soaking wet with salt water for the seas were washing over them for hours, but when he heard that me and Jimsie were so concerned about him he set off from Peterhead and tramped through the rain to set our minds at rest. It's a good eight miles from Peterhead, Mr Duncan, and I think that's a point that will stand on Sandy's side when all is counted. Well, when I was told, we went to bed again, and, as you know, none of us got to the church, for we were all worn out for want of sleep.

When Kirsty ran down with Frazer's telegraph I peeked past the blind, but didn't draw it up. Folk wondered about it, and I hear they were annoyed with us for the want of kindly feeling. But you see, our own was come home, and that was why the blind wasn't drawn up.

And I see you are going away Mr Duncan; thank you kindly for coming, and hasten you back.'

The half moon in the sky near the Hawklaw, Cruden Bay beach.

## HODDIE'S GRIEVANCE (ORIGINAL)

Hoddie was once a fisherman, and, like all the rest of the fishermen in the Ward, he had a tee name. Hoddie was his tee name, but how or why he got it I cannot tell. I dare not tell his real name, for he would be offended if, knowing his real name, I called him Hoddie. Nevertheless, should you want to find him in the village and ask for him by his real name, no one will be able to tell you where he lives, but if you ask for 'Hoddie' any 'loonie' or 'quynie' will tell you. You will do well to remember these two points when you wish to make discoveries in the Ward: first, when you are searching for a fisherman, ask for him by his tee name, and second, when you have found him, address him as mister.

One half-educated visitor made the mistake of saying 'Mr. Hoddie', and Hoddie's face grew harder than usual. It took a long time for that belated visitor to make up leeway in Hoddie's estimation, and I doubt if Hoddie ever could rise to the height of saying, 'he his a great respect fur me.' I do not know any place like the Ward where one may get such a true idea of the extent and limitation of his knowledge. M.A. B.A. B.D. and D.D. and all the well-known symbols of scholastic dignity are so much abracadabra to the Ward. They have a syllabary of their own, wherein, if ye stumble, beware of presumption. P.H.D., A.N., B.F., and K.Y. they know, and many other cabalistic characters unknown to the common schools of learning. Search for wisdom then, and above all seek understanding. Hoddie caught the Minister slipping one day, and he was deeply offended, for the slip meant a limitation of knowledge of and interest in the chief man of the Ward in the estimation of Hoddie.

One Sunday morning the whole population of the Ward was in a condition of suspense and anxiety about the boats, two of which had not been reported since the storm. Just before service the minister heard of Frazer's telegram reporting the boats safe at Aberdeen, and, in the prayer during service, he gave thanks for the good news of safety, and prayed for those yet in trouble on the sea. Next Sunday, Hoddie's seat was empty, and again for another Sunday there was no sign of Hoddie. Then a cautious old deacon said to the minister, 'if a was you a wad gyang awa doon an' see Hoddie.'

'Why is he ill?' exclaimed the minister.

'Na, he's no that ill ava,' said the deacon. 'But a'm jidgin he's no' sair pleased aboot something.'

The Minister drew his brows together thinking hard, but no light broke on his mind, and his face was troubled. At last he said, 'what can be the matter? I saw him on Saturday, and things seemed all pleasant then. Do you know anything about it?'

'A some doot it was something ye did yersel', or raither something ye didna dae, but ye better gyang an' speir.'

So the minister went that afternoon to see Hoddie. He found him sitting all alone by the fire having just finished his afternoon meal of tea, dried fish, and oatcake.

The sanded floor was plentifully sprinkled with the debris of his repast, for Hoddie followed the custom of the place, throwing the fish bones on the floor after they were clean picked with thumb and finger. As the minister entered, Hoddie reached behind him, and, drawing out from the mattress of his bed a stiff oaten straw, began to pick his teeth with it. So long as his mattress lasted, Hoddie would not lack a tooth-pick. By this act Hoddie showed one trait of the born diplomatist. It is an advantage to have something to do when engaged in delicate negotiations. A tooth-pick judiciously used gives a man a thoughtful appearance and affords time to collect wandering ideas. Many a good masculine argument is totally confounded by the rigorous click or awful pause of knitting needles in feminine hands.

'How are you today Mr. Forbes,' said the minister cheerily, on entering.

'Oh, no that ill ava, considerin': hoo's yersel'?' said Hoddie.

'I am well, thank you,' said the minister, taking a seat at Hoddie's invitation, and feeling at a loss how to begin the subject. Considering it better to plunge into the business, he summoned up courage and began, 'I am sorry you were not at Church yesterday, as I think the subject would have been interesting to you.'

'Aye, so they telt me,' said Hoddie. 'Ye was speakin' aboot Paul's shipwreck. We had a news aboot it last nicht, an' a'm some thinkin' ye war hardly stracht. A widna' min' conterin' ye on ae pint onywye.'

'Indeed!' said the minister smiling. 'What point was that? Perhaps we'll be able to come to a bearing on it.'

'I doot if we'll ever dae that,' replied Hoddie with calmly judicial face. 'But we'll hae't through han's onywye. Ye said that sailors in Bible times had to tak their coorse by the stars at nicht, an' by pints and heidlan's in daylicht. An' ye said that they daurna ventur' far frae lan', but creepit alang the coast fur they had nae compass to help them to ken fat airt tae gyang.'

'Yes,' replied the minister, wondering where this was to lead. 'I did say that, do you think it is not true?'

'True!' exclaimed Hoddie. 'Man I wunner to hear a learn't man like you, an' a minister tae, tryin' to mak fouk believe sic like.'

'Well,' replied the minister, 'I'll be glad to hear your views of the matter. Do you think the mariner's compass was in use in Europe at that time?'

'As regairds Europe,' said Hoddie with a keen look on his face, 'I canna say fur certain, I some doot it maybe wasna', but as regards Paul's ship I ken she had ane, an' I wunner ye dinna ken that.' 'See!' continued Hoddie, getting excited as he imagined the minister in a tight corner, and reaching for his Bible. 'See this book, I believe every word o't frae brod to brod, an' fat's Europe, or for that maitter, fat's Peterheid to the Scripter. See there na, Acts twenty-aicht and twalt, read that and tell me fat it says.'

The minister took the book and read, 'And landing at Syracuse we tarried there three days, and from thence we fetched a compass and came to Rhegium.'

The minister looked up and laughed, but Hoddie looked triumphant and cried, 'noo can ye conter that?'

'Well! well!' cried the minister trying to control his muscles, 'that is wonderful; I have read that many a time, but I never saw its meaning in that fashion. I am hardly prepared to believe your way of it for the phrase admits of another interpretation.'

'Phrase here or phrase there,' said Hoddie, 'ye maun believ't. It's aither true or its a lie, an' being in the word ye canna contert.'

'Then do you think that it is necessary that I should believe it according to your view of the passage?' said the minister.

'As regairds that,' said Hoddie, 'I wad say fat Skipper said anent dippin' fouk in baptism, I wadna jist haud that it's necessary, but I'll uphaud it's essential.'

'Well,' replied the minister who saw that it would be better to let Hoddie taste the sweets of victory so as to plain soften him, 'I'll think of this, and we'll have another talk about it, but I came about another matter. I hear you are offended with me for doing something of which I am ignorant: tell me what it is.'

'Div ye min' fat ye were prayin' fur that day Frazer's telegraph cam?' said Hoddie.

'Yes,' replied the minister, 'I thanked God for the good news received of the missing Ward boats, and I prayed for others not heard of.'

'Ye did that,' said Hoddie, 'an' ye did wricht, but syne ye forgat ithers at sud a been mindit as well.'

'Why!' said the minister astonished, 'I thought all the Ward boats were accounted for. What others do you mean?'

'Aye, a' the Ward boats,' said Hoddie, 'but no a' the Ward men. Did ye no ken at I had five sons fishin' oot o' Peterheid? Oor auld wife was waitin' and watchin' at the harbour heid frae Wansday tae Monday's mornin', speirin' at ilka boat at cam' in fur word o' Sandy's boat. Syne she wad gyang awa up to her gweedochters an' sit an' greet. Syne she wad be up and oot again wi' her plaid owre her heid, an' naething wad keep her frae the harbour.

She could naether eat nor sleep nor sit still, an' was sair made aboot they sons, an' deed I wasna muckle better mysel'. Hiv I no rizzon to quarrel ye for no min' in my sons, an' them belongin' to the place? I was very sair hurt, sir.'

'I am sorry,' replied the minister, 'But really I did not know about this.'

'That maks the thing a' the waur,' replied Hoddie. 'Fat hae ye deacons fur if they canna tell ye sic like?'

'But why did not you tell me yourself?' said the minister.

'A'm no a deacon,' cried Hoddie indignantly. 'Na! na ye dinna want the like o' me fur a deacon, I'm owre plain spoken, tho' fur that matter ye maybe hae waur. A deacon sud dae a deacon's work an' think something ayont's ain sel'. A'm no a man to dae work at am no appintet.'

'Then,' said the minister, 'it is the deacon you are offended with, not me.'

'Na! na sir, ye'll no win oot o' the fankle that wye. You hae yer duty tae, an' speirin' things an' takkin' a kindly interest in a' the fouk an' a' the fouk's friens. Ye wad a kent if ye'd dune that. I canna get ony blessin' in the Church fan things'r that wye. First pure, than peaceable, that's ma wye.'

'But, after all,' replied the minister, 'I did pray for your sons.'

'Fan did ye that?' said Hoddie, 'I didna heart an' I min' ilka word ye said.'

The minister replied, 'Did I not pray for all in peril on the sea?'

'Aye, ye did that,' said Hoddie. 'But let me pit a question, had ye my five sons in yer min' fan ye prayed? Na! Weel ye see, sir, ye didna pray for them. Ilka ane kent fa ye meant fan ye spak of gweed news, but naebody heard a partic'lar word aboot oor anes.'

'Well well!' said the minister, 'If I have sinned in this I am sorry and I ask your pardon. I hope I have not sinned past forgiveness.'

This humility on the minister's part, although like surrender, was in reality a flank attack. Hoddie was not prepared for it, and, as all his energies were concentrated on pushing his advantage, he could not rally himself for a change of front. He felt doubtless as many have felt when, after pursuing a boy with threats of dire punishment, the boy is unfortunately caught, and the pursuer is at a loss how to fulfil his threats. At any rate, Hoddie looked foolish, and tried to look dignified.

'Dinna beg my pardon, sir,' he said. 'I forgie ye frae a' my hert, an' syne I'll forget, but dinna dae't again.'

Main Street, Cruden Bay.

# HODDIE'S GRIEVANCE (ENGLISH)

Hoddie was once a fisherman, and, like all the rest of the fishermen in the Ward, he had a tee name. Hoddie was his tee name, but how or why he got it I cannot tell. I dare not tell his real name, for he would be offended if, knowing his real name, I called him Hoddie. Nevertheless, should you want to find him in the village and ask for him by his real name, no one will be able to tell you where he lives, but if you ask for 'Hoddie' any boy or girl will tell you. You will do well to remember these two points when you wish to make discoveries in the Ward: first, when you are searching for a fisherman, ask for him by his tee name, and second, when you have found him, address him as Mister. One half-educated visitor made the mistake of saying 'Mr. Hoddie', and Hoddie's face grew harder than usual. It took a long time for that belated visitor to make up leeway in Hoddie's estimation, and I doubt if Hoddie ever could rise to the height of saying, 'he has a great respect for me.'

I do not know any place like the Ward where one may get such a true idea of the extent and limitation of his knowledge. M.A. B.A. B.D. and D.D., and all the well-known symbols of scholastic dignity, are so much abracadabra to the Ward. They have a syllabary of their own, wherein, if you stumble, beware of presumption. P.H.D., A.N., B.F., and K.Y., [Fishing boat registration codes: P.H.D. - Peterhead: A.N. - Anstruther: B.F. – Banff, and K.Y. – Kirkcaldy.] they know, and many other cabalistic characters unknown to the common schools of learning. Search for wisdom then, and above all seek understanding. Hoddie caught the minister slipping one day, and he was deeply offended, for the slip meant a limitation of knowledge of and interest in the chief man of the Ward in the estimation of Hoddie.

One Sunday morning the whole population of the Ward was in a condition of suspense and anxiety about the boats, two of which had not been reported since the storm. Just before service, the minister heard of Frazer's telegram reporting the boats safe at Aberdeen, and, in the prayer during service, he gave thanks for the good news of safety, and prayed for those yet in trouble on the sea. Next Sunday Hoddie's seat was empty, and again for another Sunday there was no sign of Hoddie. Then a cautious old deacon said to the minister, 'if I was you I would go away down and see Hoddie.'

'Why is he ill?' exclaimed the minister.

'No, he's not that ill at all,' said the deacon. 'But I'm judging that he's not particularly pleased about something.'

The minister drew his brows together thinking hard, but no light broke on his mind, and his face was troubled. At last he said, 'What can be the matter? I saw him on Saturday, and things seemed all pleasant then. Do you know anything about it?'

'I have some doubt it was something you did, or rather something you didn't do, but you better go and enquire.'

So the minister went that afternoon to see Hoddie. He found him sitting all alone by the fire having just finished his afternoon meal of tea, dried fish, and oatcake.

The sanded floor was plentifully sprinkled with the debris of his repast, for Hoddie followed the custom of the place, throwing the fish bones on the floor after they were clean picked with thumb and finger. As the minister entered, Hoddie reached behind him, and, drawing out from the mattress of his bed a stiff oaten straw, began to pick his teeth with it. So long as his mattress lasted, Hoddie would not lack a tooth-pick. By this act Hoddie showed one trait of the born diplomatist. It is an advantage to have something to do when engaged in delicate negotiations. A tooth-pick judiciously used gives a man a thoughtful appearance and affords time to collect wandering ideas. Many a good masculine argument is totally confounded by the rigorous click or awful pause of knitting needles in feminine hands.

'How are you today Mr. Forbes,' said the minister cheerily, on entering.

'Oh, not that ill at all, considering: how's yourself?' said Hoddie.

'I am well, thank you,' said the minister, taking a seat at Hoddie's invitation, and feeling at a loss how to begin the subject. Considering it better to plunge into the business he summoned up courage and began, 'I am sorry you were not at Church yesterday, as I think the subject would have been interesting to you.'

'Aye, so they told me,' said Hoddie. 'You were speaking about Paul's shipwreck. We had a chat about it last night, and I was thinking you were hardly straight. I wouldn't mind challenging you on a point, anyway.'

'Indeed!' said the minister smiling, 'What point was that? Perhaps we'll be able to come to a bearing on it.'

'I doubt if we'll ever do that,' replied Hoddie with calmly judicial face, 'but we'll have to try anyway. You said that sailors in Bible times had to take their course by the stars at night, and by points and headland in daylight. And you said that they dare not venture far from land, but crept along the coast because they had no compass to help know which way to go.'

'Yes,' replied the minister, wondering where this was to lead. 'I did say that, do you think it is not true?'

'True!' exclaimed Hoddie, 'Man I wonder to hear an educated man like you, and a minister too, trying to make people believe this.'

'Well', replied the minister, 'I'll be glad to hear your views of the matter. Do you think the mariner's compass was in use in Europe at that time?'

'As regards Europe,' said Hoddie with a keen look on his face, 'I cannot say for certain, I have some doubt it maybe wasn't, but as regards Paul's ship I know she had one, and I wonder why you don't know that.' 'See!' continued Hoddie, getting excited as he imagined the minister in a tight corner, and reaching for his Bible. 'See this book, I believe every word of it from board to board, and what is Europe, or for that matter, what is Peterhead to the Scripture. See there now, Acts twenty-eight and twelve, read that and tell me what it says.'

The minister took the book and read, 'And landing at Syracuse we tarried there three days, and from thence we fetched a compass and came to Rhegium.' ['Fetch a compass' is an old phrase that means to go about or manoeuvre.]

The minister looked up and laughed, but Hoddie looked triumphant and cried, 'Now can you counter that?'

'Well! Well!' cried the minister trying to control his muscles, 'that is wonderful; I have read that many a time, but I never saw its meaning in that fashion. I am hardly prepared to believe your way of it for the phrase admits of another interpretation.'

'Phrase here or phrase there,' said Hoddie, 'you must believe it. It's either true or it's a lie, and being in the Bible you cannot counter it.'

'Then do you think that it is necessary that I should believe it according to your view of the passage?' said the minister.

'As regards that,' said Hoddie, 'I would say what Skipper said about dipping folk in baptism, I wouldn't hold that it's necessary, but I'll uphold it's essential.'

'Well,' replied the minister, who saw that it would be better to let Hoddie taste the sweets of victory so as to plain soften him, 'I'll think of this, and we'll have another talk about it, but I came about another matter. I hear you are offended with me for doing something of which I am ignorant: tell me what it is.'

'Do you remember what you were praying for that day Frazer's telegraph came?' said Hoddie.

'Yes,' replied the minister, 'I thanked God for the good news received of the missing Ward boats, and I prayed for others not heard of.'

'You did that,' said Hoddie, 'and you did right, but then you forgot others that should have been remembered as well.'

'Why!' said the minister astonished, 'I thought all the Ward boats were accounted for. What others do you mean?'

'Aye, all the Ward boats,' said Hoddie, 'but not all the Ward men. Did ye not know that I had five sons fishing out of Peterhead? My wife was waiting and watching at the harbour head from Wednesday to Monday morning, looking at each boat that came in for word of Sandy's boat. Then she would go away up to her daughters-in-law and sit and weep. Then she would be up and out again with her plaid over her head, and nothing would keep her from the harbour.

She could neither eat nor sleep nor sit still, and was agitated about those sons, indeed I wasn't much better myself. Have I no reason to quarrel with you for not remembering my sons, and them belonging to the place? I was extremely hurt, sir.'

'I am sorry,' replied the minister, 'But really I did not know about this.'

'That makes it all the worse,' replied Hoddie. 'What do you have deacons for if they cannot tell you things like this?'

'But why did you not tell me yourself?' said the minister.

'I am not a deacon,' cried Hoddie indignantly. 'No! No you don't want the likes of me for a deacon, I'm over plain spoken, for that matter. A deacon should do a deacon's work and think something beyond one's self. I'm not a man to do work that I am not appointed for.'

'Then,' said the minister, 'It is the deacon you are offended with, not me.'

'No! No sir, you will not get out of the trap that way. You have your duty too, and asking about things and taking a kindly interest in all the folk and folk's friends. You would know if you had done that. I cannot get any blessing in the Church when things are that way. First pure, then peaceable, that's my way.'

'But, after all,' replied the minister, 'I did pray for your sons.'

'When did you that?' said Hoddie. 'I didn't hear it and I remembered every word you said.'

The minister replied, 'Did I not pray for all in peril on the sea?'

'Aye, you did do that,' said Hoddie. 'But let me put a question, had you my five sons in your mind when you prayed? No! Well you see, sir, you didn't pray for them. Everyone knew what you meant when you spoke of good news, but nobody heard a particular word about our own ones.'

'Well well!' said the minister, 'if I have sinned in this I am sorry and I ask your pardon. I hope I have not sinned past forgiveness.'

This humility on the minister's part, although like surrender, was in reality a flank attack. Hoddie was not prepared for it, and, as all his energies were concentrated on pushing his advantage, he could not rally himself for a change of front. He felt doubtless as many have felt when, after pursuing a boy with threats of dire punishment, the boy is unfortunately caught, and the pursuer is at a loss how to fulfil his threats. At any rate, Hoddie looked foolish, and tried to look dignified.

'Don't beg my pardon, sir,' he said. 'I will forgive you from all my heart, and then I'll forget, but don't do it again.'

The fisherfolk of Port Erroll (courtesy of Jean Kelman).

Harbour Street, 1903 (courtesy of Ann Findlay).

# A CASE OF CONSCIENCE (ORIGINAL)

A conscience is an awkward possession, for, like a bicycle, it will not pack. There is no kind of compromise in a conscience. It demands so much space, yet it runs all over the place and kicks. One cannot take revenge on it, for, if it be punctured or broken, one has to push or carry the dead body.

If you drive it up hill it takes the breath from you and the desire of life: if you don't watch, it will run off with you down hill, and you are in for damages. You may train it to run in a rut, but, if you would leave the rut, it will throw you. Conscience is as uncompromising allied with blue blood as it is with the ordinary red corpuscles. The blue blood conscience has so far yielded to training that it lies under protest in one room of the palace, and gets an airing on Sundays in the House of God, or on week-days in the House of Lords when the welfare of the people has to be looked after. But, when conscience takes possession of a one-roomed house, there is a hard tussle. The Ward affords many types of character and many types of conscience, but this is one hitherto unrecorded.

The old Pilot lived in a one-roomed house: a little old house with a clay floor trodden hard: a flat stone hearth on which burned a heaped-up fire of coals. The chimney was a hanging one made of a wooden framework attached to the wall and covered over with old sailcloth, well coated with blistered whitewash.

The walls were low, and the dark lines of the rafters could be traced from wall plate to roof tree. The only ceiling was dried fish lying on the cross beams, and between the lines of fish the bare tile showed their ruddy sides. A table, a cupboard, a box-bed with doors to shut, three chairs each split across the seat, a little hanging shelf covered with wall paper, on which reposed a few dingy books, made up the furniture. For ornament, a grocer's calendar, a highly coloured chart of the ways of life and death in Chinese perspective, and a Roman Catholic impression in glaring tints of the Adoration of the Virgin, sufficed together with what sunlight penetrated the little square window. From the dusky shadows of the box-bed gleamed a pair of dark, beady eyes, set deep under black bushy eyebrows. The face to which they belonged was strong and heavy of feature, dark, seamed, and full of a sphinx-like quality that seemed to defy entreaty. It looked a hard face, one that could front fate impassive. There seemed to be no yield in it.

He had a son and three daughters living, yet he lived all alone and refused assistance. His only means of subsistence was the pittance he received as pilot of the little steamer that visited the Ward at intervals. It was not a case of quarrel, but a 'Case of Conscience'.

'The children shall not lay up for the fathers, but the fathers for the children' is a word that held him fast. He was invulnerable, like Balder the beautiful, except at one point and by one weapon. Balder was vulnerable in the head, and the fatal weapon was a branch of mistletoe. The old Pilot's soft place was what seemed the hardest, his heart, and a little child was the besieger. His little grandson could do no harm: he was absolutely perfect, and, like the rest of grandfathers, or rather grandmothers, the old man lost no opportunity of spoiling the Jewel. His affection, restrained from his own children, flooded the child. But this is not the story. This only points to the fact that the old man had a heart as well as a conscience, and both were eccentric. He had fallen on evil days, for he was deaf as a post, and he had a 'Hoast an' a spit'. Few visited him, for few could speak to him. One's words must be carefully selected and parsimonious in syllables when speaking to the deaf, and a cheerful remark on the weather is as much out of place as it would be at a Council of State.

'Well, how are you today?' cried the minister into one ear clear of blankets.

'Aye it's a fine day,' responded the old man in muffled voice.

'Yes, it's a beautiful day,' assented the minister, making the best of the situation.

'Fat say ye?' cried the old Pilot raising himself on his elbow.

'It's a fine day,' reiterated the minister, feeling the words somewhat commonplace on repetition.

'Aye, that's fat a was sayin',' said the old man, looking somewhat fierce as if his word was doubted, for when you bawl, the words may either convey assertion or question.

'Is your cold better?' the minister then cried, to change the subject.

'Aye, some,' said the old man, 'but a wadna care aboot the cauld, it's the hoast that flegs me.'

'When your cold goes the coughing will stop,' cried the minister.

'I didna say naething aboot a coffin,' said the Pilot, 'it's a hoast an' a spit.'

'Will nothing help it,' cried the minister.

'Na, naething; it's no-like ony ither hoast, an' the spit cow'rs the doctor. Fan a lie doon at nicht a hoast an' hoast an' it comes up: syne fan fower o'clock comes it chinges an' syne it comes doon frae ma heid. It's a sair hoast, an' the doctor his nae bottle for't.'

The minister had no prescription for such a case; he saw that it was one of those obscure Ward troubles that succumb only to time and miracle. But he set about extemporising an ear trumpet when he got home, against his next visit. The end of a trumpet formed the bell; a short length of bamboo, terminating in a piece of rubber tube with ear piece attached, made up the instrument.

When the minister called, the old Pilot was seated at the fire. The trumpet was produced, and he gazed at it with his little eyes agleam. Turning it curiously in his hands he said, 'Fat am a to do wi' this?' and, putting the ear piece into his mouth he blew into it.

'No, no,' cried the minister laughing, 'put it in your ear.' He did so with some trepidation, and the minister, putting his mouth to the bell end, said, 'How are you today? Do you hear me?'

'Aye, a hear ye fine. That's a wunner. As well's ever a hear't in ma life. Fat's in't ava? Far gat ye't? Speak again,' he said.

'I made it for you,' said the minister. 'I want to have a talk with you.'

'Ye made it yersel'; weel, ye'r a skeely ane.'

Then ensued a conversation, the subject matter of which does not enter into this story, and, after prayer through the trumpet, the old man was left well pleased in possession of his ear horn. All things looked well for a series of such talks, but here conscience played one of her tricks and upset all plans. It happened that, while the minister's horn was being made, a gentleman at the castle, who visited the old Pilot, had sent to London for an ear horn of the newest pattern. When he took his instrument to the old man, he found the minister's in effective occupation.

After a conversation by means of the new horn, the gentleman left it in possession of the old pilot. It is not an uncommon experience to witness a lively conscience caused by a perplexing increase of property. Deafness is not only a deprivation: it is also a defence. The sweet sounds of the world are lost indeed on the deaf ear, but the deaf ear defies the bitter sounds. I fancy the old man felt as China did when both Germany and Russia were poking their ear horns into either side of the head, breaking up the isolation of centuries, and, like China, the old Pilot might wish to please both, and felt it impossible. Be that as it may, when the minister called, his composite horn was placed in his hands, not to speak through, but to carry home again. 'I canna ase't ony mair, Sir, it hurts ma heid. Na! ye needna try't, a canna hear wi't ava. It sets ma heid a' birrin' an' jum'lin'.'

'But you heard well enough last time,' cried the minister. 'Let us try it again.'

'Na! na! I'll no hae nane o't, it's ane o' thae inventions at we hear tell o' in the word.'

'What do you refer to?' said the minister. 'Some place it says "God made man upright, but they have sought out many inventions". Na! if the Lord means me to hear he'll lat me hear, but that gyangs conter to His will.'

'When did it begin to hurt your head?' said the minister quite perplexed.

'Well ye see, the Captain fess't me a horn an' spak to me, but I didna hear sae weel as wi' yours. It was his horn at did it, an' syne a canna hear wi' nane.'

'Let me see the new horn,' said the minister. 'You ought to use it when he was so kind as to get it for you. Then he can talk to you when he comes.'

'I kenna far it is,' said the old man querulously. 'Na, I'll nae fess't oot, a canna bide the look o't: an' ye'l jist tak' yer ain bonnie trumpet awa hame wi' ye. It might be the Lord's wull to hear you through this ane ian ye speak gweed words to me an' pit up a prayer, but it canna be vricht to ase sic like newsin' like, as the Captain dis aboot or'nary maitters. Jist tak it awa hame na, like a kin' gentleman an' lat me bide the Lord's will.'

There was no appeal against that judgment, so the horn was taken home, and the old pilot sat till the end came in his silent world. Since that time the old pilot has gone home, and one at least who knew him believes that:

> 'He met his Pilot face to face
> When he had crossed the bar.'

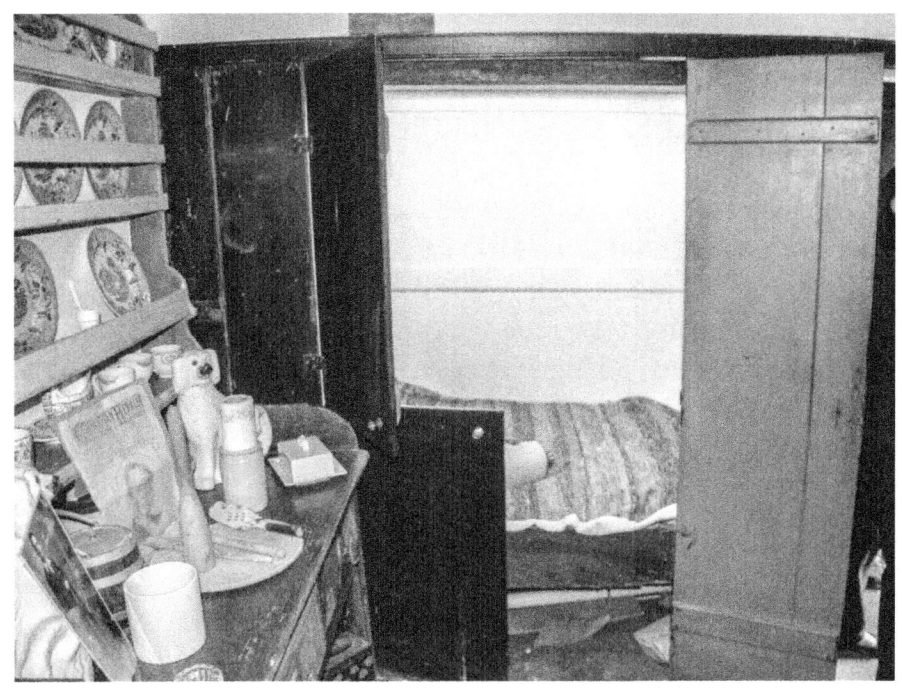
Box bed. Maggie's Hoose, Cairnbulg, Aberdeenshire.

## A CASE OF CONSCIENCE (ENGLISH)

A conscience is an awkward possession, for, like a bicycle, it will not pack. There is no kind of compromise in a conscience. It demands so much space, yet it runs all over the place and kicks. One cannot take revenge on it, for, if it be punctured or broken, one has to push or carry the dead body.

If you drive it up hill it takes the breath from you and the desire of life: if you don't watch, it will run off with you down hill, and you are in for damages. You may train it to run in a rut, but, if you would leave the rut, it will throw you. Conscience is as uncompromising allied with blue blood as it is with the ordinary red corpuscles. The blue blood conscience has so far yielded to training that it lies under protest in one room of the palace, and gets an airing on Sundays in the House of God, or on week-days in the House of Lords when the welfare of the people has to be looked after. But, when conscience takes possession of a one-roomed house, there is a hard tussle. The Ward affords many types of character and many types of conscience, but this is one hitherto unrecorded.

The old Pilot lived in a one-roomed house: a little old house with a clay floor trodden hard: a flat stone hearth on which burned a heaped-up fire of coals. The chimney was a hanging one made of a wooden framework attached to the wall and covered over with old sailcloth, well coated with blistered whitewash.

The walls were low, and the dark lines of the rafters could be traced from wall plate to roof tree. The only ceiling was dried fish lying on the cross beams, and between the lines of fish the bare tile showed their ruddy sides. A table, a cupboard, a box-bed with doors to shut, three chairs each split across the seat, a little hanging shelf covered with wall paper, on which reposed a few dingy books, made up the furniture. For ornament, a grocer's calendar, a highly coloured chart of the ways of life and death in Chinese perspective, and a Roman Catholic impression in glaring tints of the Adoration of the Virgin, sufficed together with what sunlight penetrated the little square window. From the dusky shadows of the box-bed gleamed a pair of dark, beady eyes, set deep under black bushy eyebrows. The face to which they belonged was strong and heavy of feature, dark, seamed, and full of a sphinx-like quality that seemed to defy entreaty. It looked a hard face, one that could front fate impassive. There seemed to be no yield in it.

He had a son and three daughters living, yet he lived all alone and refused assistance. His only means of subsistence was the pittance he received as pilot of the little steamer that visited the Ward at intervals. It was not a case of quarrel, but a 'Case of Conscience'.

'The children shall not lay up for the fathers, but the fathers for the children' is a word that held him fast. He was invulnerable, like Balder the beautiful, except at one point and by one weapon. Balder was vulnerable in the head, and the fatal weapon was a branch of mistletoe. The old Pilot's soft place was what seemed the hardest, his heart, and a little child was the besieger. His little grandson could do no harm: he was absolutely perfect, and, like the rest of grandfathers, or rather grandmothers, the old man lost no opportunity of spoiling the Jewel. His affection, restrained from his own children, flooded the child. But this is not the story. This only points to the fact that the old man had a heart as well as a conscience, and both were eccentric. He had fallen on evil days, for he was deaf as a post, and he had a 'cough and a spit'. Few visited him, for few could speak to him. One's words must be carefully selected and parsimonious in syllables when speaking to the deaf, and a cheerful remark on the weather is as much out of place as it would be at a Council of State.

'Well, how are you today?' cried the minister into one ear clear of blankets.

'Aye it's a fine day,' responded the old man in muffled voice.

'Yes, it's a beautiful day,' assented the minister, making the best of the situation.

'What did you say?' cried the old Pilot raising himself on his elbow.

'It's a fine day,' reiterated the minister, feeling the words somewhat commonplace on repetition.

'Aye, that's what I was saying,' said the old man, looking somewhat fierce as if his word was doubted, for when you bawl, the words may either convey assertion or question.

'Is your cold better?' the minister then cried, to change the subject.

'Aye, some,' said the old man. 'But I wouldn't care about the cold; it's the cough that scares me.'

'When your cold goes the coughing will stop,' cried the minister. 'I didn't say anything about a coffin,' said the Pilot. 'It's a cough and a spit.'

'Will nothing help it,' cried the minister.

'No, nothing; it's not like any other cough, and the spit worries the doctor. When I lie down at night I cough and cough and it comes up: after four o'clock it changes and then it comes down from my head. It's a sore cough, and the doctor has no bottle for it.'

The minister had no prescription for such a case; he saw that it was one of those obscure Ward troubles that succumb only to time and miracle. But he set about extemporising an ear trumpet when he got home, against his next visit. The end of a trumpet formed the bell; a short length of bamboo, terminating in a piece of rubber tube with ear piece attached, made up the instrument.

When the minister called the old Pilot was seated at the fire. The trumpet was produced, and he gazed at it with his little eyes agleam. Turning it curiously in his hands he said, 'What am I to do with this?' and, putting the ear piece into his mouth, he blew into it.

'No, no,' cried the minister laughing, 'put it in your ear'. He did so with some trepidation, and the minister, putting his mouth to the bell end, said, 'How are you today? Do you hear me?'

'Aye, I hear you fine. That's a wonder. As well as ever I've heard in my life. What is in it? Where did you get it? Speak again,' he said.

'I made it for you,' said the minister: 'I want to have a talk with you.'

'You made it yourself; well, you are a skilled one.'

Then ensued a conversation, the subject matter of which does not enter into this story, and, after prayer through the trumpet, the old man was left well pleased in possession of his ear horn. All things looked well for a series of such talks, but here conscience played one of her tricks and upset all plans. It happened that, while the minister's horn was being made, a gentleman at the castle [Captain Webbe, husband of the earl's older sister, Lady Cecilia], who visited the old Pilot, had sent to London for an ear horn of the newest pattern. When he took his instrument to the old man, he found the minister's in effective occupation.

After a conversation by means of the new horn, the gentleman left it in possession of the old pilot. It is not an uncommon experience to witness a lively conscience caused by a perplexing increase of property. Deafness is not only a deprivation: it is also a defence. The sweet sounds of the world are lost indeed on the deaf ear, but the deaf ear defies the bitter sounds. I fancy the old man felt as China did when both Germany and Russia were poking their ear horns into either side of the head, breaking up the isolation of centuries, and, like China, the old Pilot might wish to please both, and felt it impossible. Be that as it may, when the minister called, his composite horn was placed in his hands, not to speak through, but to carry home again.

'I cannot use it any more, Sir, it hurts my head. No! You needn't try it, I cannot hear with it at all. It makes my head dizzy and muddled.'

'But you heard well enough last time,' cried the minister. 'Let us try it again.'

'No! No! I won't have any of it; it's one of those inventions that we hear about in the Bible.'

'What do you refer to?' said the minister.

'Some place it says "God made man upright, but they have sought out many inventions. No! If the Lord means me to hear he'll let me hear, but that goes counter to His will".'

'When did it begin to hurt your head?' said the minister quite perplexed.

'Well you see, the Captain fetched me a horn and spoke to me, but I didn't hear so well as with yours. It was his horn that did it, and ever since I cannot hear with one.'

'Let me see the new horn,' said the minister. 'You ought to use it when he was so kind as to get it for you. Then he can talk to you when he comes.'

'I don't know where it is,' said the old man querulously. 'No: I will not get it. I cannot stand the look of it: and you will just take your own bonnie trumpet away home with you. It might be the Lord's will to hear you through this one since you speak good words to me and put up a prayer, but it cannot be right to use it for gossiping, as the Captain does about ordinary matters. Just take it away home like a kind gentleman and let me honour the Lord's will.'

There was no appeal against that judgment, so the horn was taken home, and the old pilot sat till the end came in his silent world. Since that time the old pilot has gone home, and one at least who knew him believes that:

'He met his Pilot face to face
When he had crossed the bar.'

[From Tennyson's *Crossing the Bar*, which compares death to a sea journey. The bar crossed is where a river enters the ocean. The full poem:

Sunset and evening star,
And one clear call for me!

And may there be no moaning of the bar,
   When I put out to sea,

  But such a tide as moving seems asleep,
   Too full for sound and foam,
When that which drew from out the boundless deep
   Turns again home.

  Twilight and evening bell,
   And after that the dark!
And may there be no sadness of farewell,
   When I embark;

  For tho' from out our bourne of Time and Place
   The flood may bear me far,
I hope to see my Pilot face to face
   When I have crost the bar.]

# STUMPIE'S PROPOSAL (ORIGINAL)

Stumpie was short and stout of frame, and short and slow of speech. He was worth looking at in his holiday rig as he paraded the main street of the Ward. His red curls crowned with a blue cap, with its straight peak set at an angle, showed an artfully careless fringe. His thick rig and fur jersey, tucked into his trousers, gave him a great breadth of beam amidships. His trousers of thick blue cloth were suspended by blue and red striped braces, shown to advantage over his jersey. His limbs terminated in a pair of shiny 'short tops' whose heels dug into the village street with the emphasis of perfect dogmatism. His whole get up, erect head, adorned with a short cutty whose bowl lay close to his cheek; gracefully curving limbs and sturdy step gave one the impression of buoyant happiness. But Stumpie was not quite happy. There was room for care under his ample jersey.

He was a man of few words. If one saluted him 'Good Morning!' his face lighted up with a smile, but he was three steps away before his hesitating 'Aye' was heard. You can imagine that such a man would have trouble if he had something special to say to some special person.

One night he wandered in a restless mood up to the coastguard watchhouse on the sea braes. The night was dark and the watchhouse untenanted, so he groped his way through the fence to the lee of the house. A voice challenged him out of the darkness:

'Faa's there? Is that you feyther?'

'No, it's me,' said Stumpie hastily but firmly, for with the shock of the unexpected came the quiet pleasure of a familiar voice. 'Fat are ye doin' here Maggie?' he cried.

'Oh I cam' up to look oot for Dave: he's comin' wi' the steamerie; the pilot said she might get in this tide. Isna' that a light ayont the Skares, Stumpie?'

'Aye it's a licht, an' a steamer's tae: ye've gweed een Maggie.'

'What for no,' she retorted, 'I'm nae that aul' yet Stumpie.'

'Na, but ye're nae sae young as ye war ance Maggie.'

The girl turned her head. 'Oh man Stumpie, speak sense, onybody can say that aboot onybody.'

He gazed intently at the dark form of the girl whose head and shoulders were shrouded in a shawl. He could not see her face, but he knew that a curl of her wayward hair fluttered in the wind, and her red lips were as saucy as ever under the shawl. As boy and girl they had known each other, had grubbed among the rocky shallows for whelks and partans, and scrambled for sand eels along the sea margins. A frank healthy comradeship had grown with their growth, and it had always been easy to tell Maggie anything until now when he was tongue-tied and so eager to speak. A step sounded on the shingly walk. Maggie started, pressed close to Stumpie, and, clinging to his arm, said, 'Oh Stumpie, fat's that, I'm feart, tak' me hame.'

The rattle of a key in a lock told Stumpie that it was only the coastguard returned to his watch, but he only said, 'Come Maggie,' and, walking on the soft grass, they escaped the notice of the man.

'Oh I'm gled he didna see us,' said Maggie as they sped homeward.

'Same here,' said Stumpie. 'But Maggie, I'm to tell ye something.'

'What is't than? Is't aboot yersel' or me?'

'It's aboot's baith,' said Stumpie gathering courage.

'Weel, tell't quick,' said Maggie, 'for I see feyther at the door lookin' for me.'

'I jist want ae thing to mak…' But here Stumpie stopped.

Maggie looked at his bashful face with remarkably unconscious eyes and said, 'To mak' what, Stumpie?'

'I jist want ae thing,' repeated Stumpie, 'jist a poun' note tae mak' a hunner.'

'Keep's a',' laughed Maggie. 'Is that a'? Hae ye nocht else. That's aboot yersel' Stumpie.'

'Aye, but it's aboot you tae Maggie, for I wad like gran'... it wad be fine... to hae the even hunner.'

Maggie laughed again. 'Deed aye it wad be gran'. If I had the half o't I wad get a polisman to keep it for me. Guid nicht Stumpie, an' thenk ye, here's feyther waitin for me.'

One warm Spring night they sat together on a bent-crowned sand hill overlooking the bay. Maggie sat somewhat downcast knitting a stocking, but Stumpie was in good spirits.

'It's a fine nicht Maggie; ane could sit lang eneuch here 'cep' for anes lines at no't to be redd.'

'Hae ye mony to dae yet?' Maggie asked quietly, her eyes intent on her knitting.

'Aye hiv I! I wrocht for fower 'oors on twa 'at were sair fanklet, an' mither said she wad feenish them. I hae ane to do fan I get hame. Dae ye see that deuks amo' the rocks Maggie? I wad as sune be a deuk as redd fanklet lines.'

'Peer folk sud be gled o' ony wye o' doin,' Maggie said, 'an' gled fan they can bide at hame amo' their ain folks. Ye didna ken I was gaun awa Stumpie?'

'No!' cried Stumpie, quite startled. 'You gaun awa? Far are ye gaun Maggie?'

Maggie lifted her eyes and looking at him said, 'Dave's gaun to Sheetland to the herrin', an' I'm gaun tae. Ane maun dae something for theirsel'. We wad a been awa a fylie syne but we want a man.'

Stumpie grew quite excited. He had never been out of the Ward, and the pleasure of seeing strange lands with Maggie not far away was very tempting.

'Ye want a man!' he cried, 'wad I dae? Will ye tak's Maggie?'

There was a curious gleam in Maggie's eyes as she rose to her feet and said: 'I wad like fine Stumpie, but we'll speer at feyther.'

Arrived at the house Maggie invited Stumpie to go in. She led him by the hand to her father, and said with a faint blush on her face: 'I'm nae gaun to Sheetland feyther, Stumpie has socht me.'

And Stumpie never could redd the fankles of that line which Maggie cast.

These granite blocks are what remains of the coastguard watch-house on Ward Hill. The watch-house is also mentioned by Bram Stoker in his novel *The Watter's Mou'*.

## STUMPIE'S PROPOSAL (ENGLISH)

Stumpie was short and stout of frame, and short and slow of speech. He was worth looking at in his holiday rig as he paraded the main street of the Ward. His red curls crowned with a blue cap, with its straight peak set at an angle, showed an artfully careless fringe. His thick rig and fur jersey, tucked into his trousers, gave him a great breadth of beam amidships. His trousers of thick blue cloth were suspended by blue and red striped braces, shown to advantage over his jersey. His limbs terminated in a pair of shiny 'short tops' whose heels dug into the village street with the emphasis of perfect dogmatism. His whole get up, erect head, adorned with a short cutty whose bowl lay close to his cheek; gracefully curving limbs and sturdy step gave one the impression of buoyant happiness. But Stumpie was not quite happy. There was room for care under his ample jersey.

He was a man of few words. If one saluted him 'Good Morning!' his face lighted up with a smile, but he was three steps away before his hesitating 'Aye' was heard. You can imagine that such a man would have trouble if he had something special to say to some special person.

One night he wandered in a restless mood up to the coastguard watch house on the sea braes. The night was dark and the watch house untenanted, so he groped his way through the fence to the lee of the house. A voice challenged him out of the darkness:

'Who's there? Is that you father?'

'No, it's me,' said Stumpie hastily but firmly, for with the shock of the unexpected came the quiet pleasure of a familiar voice. 'What are you doing here Maggie?' he cried.

'Oh I came up to look out for Dave: he's coming with the steamer; the pilot said she might get in this tide. Isn't that a light beyond the Skares, Stumpie?'

'Aye it's a light, and' a steamer's it is too: you have good eyes Maggie.'

'What for now,' she retorted, 'I'm not that old yet Stumpie.'

'No, but you are not so young as you were once Maggie.'

The girl turned her head. 'Oh man Stumpie, speak sense, anybody can say that about anybody.'

He gazed intently at the dark form of the girl whose head and shoulders were shrouded in a shawl. He could not see her face, but he knew that a curl of her wayward hair fluttered in the wind, and her red lips were as saucy as ever under the shawl. As boy and girl they had known each other, had grubbed among the rocky shallows for whelks and crabs, and scrambled for sand eels along the sea margins. A frank healthy comradeship had grown with their growth, and it had always been easy to tell Maggie anything until now when he was tongue-tied and so eager to speak. A step sounded on the shingly walk. Maggie started, pressed close to Stumpie, and, clinging to his arm, said, 'Oh Stumpie, what's that, I'm scared, take me home.'

The rattle of a key in a lock told Stumpie that it was only the coastguard returned to his watch, but he only said, 'Come Maggie,' and, walking on the soft grass, they escaped the notice of the man.

'Oh I'm glad he didn't see us,' said Maggie as they sped homeward.

'Same here,' said Stumpie. 'But Maggie, I'm going to tell you something.'

'What is it then? Is it about yourself or me?'

'It's about us both,' said Stumpie gathering courage.

'Well, tell it quick,' said Maggie, 'for I see father at the door looking for me.'

'I just want one thing to make...' But here Stumpie stopped.

Maggie looked at his bashful face with remarkably unconscious eyes and said, 'To make what, Stumpie?'

'I just want one thing,' repeated Stumpie, 'just a pound note to make a hundred.'

'What,' laughed Maggie. 'Is that all? Have you nothing else to say. That's about yourself Stumpie.'

'Aye, but it's about you too Maggie, for I would like very much... it would be fine... to have the even hundred.'

Maggie laughed again. 'Indeed yes it would be grand. If I had the half of it I would get a policeman to keep it for me. Good night Stumpie, and thank you, here's father waiting for me.'

One warm spring night they sat together on a bent-crowned sand hill overlooking the bay. Maggie sat somewhat downcast knitting a stocking, but Stumpie was in good spirits.

'It's a fine night Maggie; one could sit long enough here except for those fishing lines that need to be untangled.'

'Have you many to do yet?' Maggie asked quietly, her eyes intent on her knitting.

'Oh yes! I worked for four hours on two that were badly tangled, and mother said she would finish them. I have one to do when I get home. Do you see those ducks amongst the rocks Maggie? I would as soon be a duck as untangle twisted lines.'

'Poor folk should be glad of any work,' Maggie said, 'and glad when they can stay at home amongst their own folks. Did you know I was going away Stumpie?'

'No!' cried Stumpie, quite startled. 'You are going away? Where are you going Maggie?'

Maggie lifted her eyes and looking at him said, 'Dave's going to Shetland to the herring, and I'm going too. One must do something for yourself. We would have been away sooner but we need a man to help out.'

Stumpie grew quite excited. He had never been out of the Ward, and the pleasure of seeing strange lands with Maggie not far away was very tempting.

'You want a man!' he cried, 'would I do? Will you take me Maggie?'

There was a curious gleam in Maggie's eyes as she rose to her feet and said: 'I would like well enough Stumpie, but we'll ask father.' Arrived at the house Maggie invited Stumpie to go in. She led him by the hand to her father, and said with a faint blush on her face: 'I'm not going to Shetland father, Stumpie has proposed to me.'

And Stumpie never could untangle the tangles of that line which Maggie cast.

## THE WRECK OF THE PEARL (ORIGINAL)

The *Pearl* was a French fishing schooner from Dunkirk going north to the Iceland cod fishing with a crew of seventeen all told.

The Ward Bay is a deadly trap for strange craft, and none that got into it with an inshore wind ever got out of it without scathe. How the Pearl got in has never been explained to men who knew the Coast. A fresh wind was blowing from the Nor' East, and the Bay was noisy and white with its endless crescents of white broken water roaring and tumbling in on the sands, but no danger was apprehended. The Ward was asleep, and even the coastguard had left his watch.

About midnight a restless fisherman heard strange sounds through the soughing of the wind, and raised the alarm that a ship was on the sands. Then the Ward awoke; lights appeared in little square windows; sounds of running feet were heard, and the hoarse voices of men mingling with the shriller tones of women as the alarm ran up the village street. One burly form stopped at Duthie's window, and, rapping loudly on the glass, called out, 'Lifeboat Coxwain, a ship on the sands.'

Then Duthie's nightcap appeared at the door, and a voice, 'Chap up the crew man Towie, an' sen' ane owre for the horses a'l be wi' ye in a meenit.'

Soon Duthie is speeding down to the Lifeboat house, passing the coastguard who is charging his alarm signal for the crew of the Life-saving Apparatus under his charge. All is bustle and excitement around him, but, as the warning shot is heard, his crew arrive by twos and threes and fall into their places. Meanwhile, across the broken water, in the pauses of wind and surf roaring, come loud distressful cries from the shipwrecked crew, whose vessel cannot be seen through the murky night. Strange sounds they seemed coming out of the darkness, sounds between laughing and crying, and anon between cursing and blessing, and the thundering surf lent its awful diapason to the incoherent treble of their prayer. No word was understood, yet distress has a common tongue, and a flare light was burned to assure them that help was coming. Along the village street the heavy cart rumbled with a bodyguard of fishermen carrying lanterns, across the river and through the weird shadows of the sandhills down to the sea. Crowds of women and children follow to the sands, for the village is now awake.

'There she is,' cried Dyson as he descried a long dark shadow lying in the broken water about 150 yards from the shore.

'Her foremast's doon,' shouted Stumpie, whose young eyes saw clearer than Dyson's. 'She's lyin' a wricht, there's nae fear o' her evenoo: a kenna fat their rarin' at.'

Her foremast had parted when she struck, carrying spars and rigging over the bow. She lay in a soft bed, and the hull was none the worse, but the crew were frantic as the seas broke over her stern and thumped the wreckage on her sides.

There was no immediate danger save in their own uncontrolled passions, but that made the tragedy all the more awful and pitiful to those who knew. But, see! The rocket is ready for firing, and the men stand at their posts. Jay stoops and applies the light, and with a hissing shriek the projectile streams high in a brilliant parabola of sparks drawing the line right over the schooner bows amid loud cheers from the crowd on shore. It was a good shot, well aimed and effective, for that line equally well used meant safety to every man aboard.

But alas! that I should have to tell the story. While the Lifesaving crew are rejoicing, a dreadful scene is being enacted aboard the schooner. Like a pack of hungry hounds the crew haul in the line with the block and 'endless faulds rope' attached; only one man knows what to do with it, and his advice is howled down. As soon as they thought they had enough rope hauled, one man was tied into it round the waist and tossed into the sea, and a lantern was dipped as a signal to haul ashore. Meanwhile, the men ashore were waiting till the hawser should be fixed, and wondering at the delay. George Milne stood thigh deep in the surf holding the rope, and Gordon Smith's sturdy figure a few paces behind him ready to haul at the signal.

'I kenna fat they're taiglin' at Gordon,' said George impatiently. 'In ma min' o't they're either feels or fuskayt.'

'They're foreigners I'm thinkin',' replied Gordon, 'an' dinna ken fat to do in the tow - Frenchmen are peer feel craters.'

'Oh man but they're signallin' haul.'

'Na Gordon, it canna be that they hivna fastened the block yet.'

Peering through the darkness these two men tried to discern the movements of the crew, and neither could see any sign of intelligent purpose. Still the lantern dipped, and now as if held by a hasty hand in spasmodic jerks that seemed to say, 'Hasten for the love of God'.

'Pu' the rope Geordie an' see gin ocht's haudin't.'

George cautiously did as Gordon desired, and, feeling a weight, he signalled to haul. All at once he seemed to stagger and shiver, then called out, 'Stop men stop, they're something wrang.'

'Fat is't ava, Geordie?'

'Come here Gordon, for God's sake.'

Gordon waded up to his companion, who said in awestruck voice, 'Something struck me evenoo Gordon an' syne twined aboot my leg. Pit doon yer haun man an' see fat it is. I daurna dae't, a'm fair fleggit.'

Gordon put down his hand in silence, then started as if he had been stung. His face was working with strong emotion as he looked up to George Milne, and the faint light of early dawn fell on his strong rugged features.

'Fat is't ava, Gordon man? Can ye no tell's?'

'It's a deid man Geordie; his tae airm's roon yer leg.'

Gordon's heart was big and tender, and the tears ran over his cheeks as, lifting the dead man gently, he said, 'Drount like a rotten in a trap peer chap , an' him but a young fallow.'

Then he rose to his full height, and, with clenched fist

shaken towards the vessel he relieved his feelings in a burst of indignation that did honour to his nature.

Little did he and his companions know that, at the other end of that fatal line, four men were tied by the waist even as this one was. Four men struggling, gasping, fighting with death, tossed among the wreckage of their own ship. Yet so it was, for in the wild frenzy of the time and in gross ignorance of the means of safety four of the crew had been tied on the line as soon as the first was hauled away. The Captain tied his own son into it, but on his cries for help he had again been hauled aboard, dozed with brandy, and put in the cabin half drowned. George Milne and Gordon Smith carried the dead man ashore, and, as they laid their burden gently on the sands amid the pitiful ejaculations of the crowd, George said, 'It's nae use this wark: they dinna ken fat they're doin': we maun hae the Life Boat. A kenna fat's come o' Duthie.'

Most of Duthie's crew had run to the sands, and he had hard work to come at volunteers, but now he was seen in the grey light carefully steering his craft towards the wreck. On board the ship the excitement was intense, and it was increased as the lifeboat approached. Two of their mates had been hauled aboard again and laid on deck, but on sight of the Life Boat the other two were forgotten. Ten men stood ready to spring into the boat as soon as she came near. Warning cries arose from Duthie and his crew, when they saw their intention, but the cries fell on deaf ears, and the ten sprang simultaneously into the boat, nearly capsizing her in their mad rush. A perfect babble of shouts and curses in a rough French patois rang out on the night winds as they staggered about impeding the men who would save them. One man persisted in thwarting the efforts of one of the crew who was fending the boat, and he was rendered quiet by a blow that stretched him in the bottom. The boat sheered off safely and landed them all on the sands. The Captain evidently expected to meet his three mates alive and well, and when he saw only one dead man he ran to the life line, held up two fingers, pointed to the ship, and made as if he would haul the line.

The men hauled with a will, and soon two dark forms appeared in the surf - the bodies of two drowned men. With pitiful cries the rescued men threw themselves on the bodies, eagerly placing their hands over their hearts, seeking for signs of life. Less attention a little earlier would have saved their lives. Then Duthie shouted from the lifeboat, 'Are ye a' there? Speer at the Captain gin ony mair's on the wreck.'

With signs the Captain was made aware of Duthie's question, and he gave a start when he comprehended. He had forgotten his own boy in the cabin. He held up three fingers, and urged them off to the ship. On board they found two men lying on deck, one dead, one with faint signs of life. In the cabin the Captain's boy lay unconscious. They brought them ashore, and on the bare sand hills they tried to restore animation to the one who showed signs of life, but it was all in vain. Thus a ghastly roll call of five dead men was the result of stupidity, ignorance, and frenzy. These five were laid in the little village hall, and the Captain's boy found a warm bed and effectual nursing from a kind-hearted fisherman's wife.

The Mission Hall, Harbour Street.

Testing the Board of Trade Life Saving Apparatus on Ward Hill (courtesy of Brian Watt).

## THE WRECK OF THE PEARL (ENGLISH)

The *Pearl* was a French fishing schooner from Dunkirk going north to the Iceland cod fishing with a crew of seventeen all told.

The Ward Bay is a deadly trap for strange craft, and none that got into it with an inshore wind ever got out of it without scathe. How the Pearl got in has never been explained to men who knew the coast. A fresh wind was blowing from the Nor' East, and the bay was noisy and white with its endless crescents of white broken water roaring and tumbling in on the sands, but no danger was apprehended. The Ward was asleep, and even the coastguard had left his watch.

About midnight a restless fisherman heard strange sounds through the soughing of the wind, and raised the alarm that a ship was on the sands. Then the Ward awoke; lights appeared in little square windows; sounds of running feet were heard, and the hoarse voices of men mingling with the shriller tones of women as the alarm ran up the village street. One burly form stopped at Duthie's window, and, rapping loudly on the glass, called out, 'Lifeboat Coxwain, a ship on the sands.'

Then Duthie's nightcap appeared at the door, and a voice, 'Knock on the doors for the crew Towie, and send one over for the horses I will be with you in a minute.'

Soon Duthie is speeding down to the Lifeboat house, passing the coastguard who is charging his alarm signal for the crew of the Life-saving Apparatus under his charge. All is bustle and excitement around him, but, as the warning shot is heard, his crew arrive by twos and threes and fall into their places. Meanwhile, across the broken water, in the pauses of wind and surf roaring, come loud distressful cries from the shipwrecked crew, whose vessel cannot be seen through the murky night. Strange sounds they seemed coming out of the darkness, sounds between laughing and crying, and anon between cursing and blessing, and the thundering surf lent its awful diapason to the incoherent treble of their prayer. No word was understood, yet distress has a common tongue, and a flare light was burned to assure them that help was coming. Along the village street the heavy cart rumbled with a bodyguard of fishermen carrying lanterns, across the river and through the weird shadows of the sandhills down to the sea. Crowds of women and children follow to the sands, for the village is now awake.

'There she is,' cried Dyson as he descried a long dark shadow lying in the broken water about 150 yards from the shore.

'Her foremast is down,' shouted Stumpie, whose young eyes saw clearer than Dyson's. 'She's lying all right, they are safe enough now: I don't know what they are shouting about.'

Her foremast had parted when she struck, carrying spars and rigging over the bow. She lay in a soft bed, and the hull was none the worse, but the crew were frantic as the seas broke over her stern and thumped the wreckage on her sides.

There was no immediate danger save in their own uncontrolled passions, but that made the tragedy all the more awful and pitiful to those who knew. But, see! The rocket is ready for firing, and the men stand at their posts. Jay stoops and applies the light, and with a hissing shriek the projectile streams high in a brilliant parabola of sparks drawing the line right over the schooner bows amid loud cheers from the crowd on shore. It was a good shot, well aimed and effective, for that line equally well used meant safety to every man aboard.

But alas! That I should have to tell the story. While the Lifesaving crew are rejoicing, a dreadful scene is being enacted aboard the schooner. Like a pack of hungry hounds the crew haul in the line with the block and 'endless faulds rope' attached; only one man knows what to do with it, and his advice is howled down. As soon as they thought they had enough rope hauled, one man was tied into it round the waist and tossed into the sea, and a lantern was dipped as a signal to haul ashore. Meanwhile, the men ashore were waiting till the hawser should be fixed, and wondering at the delay. George Milne stood thigh deep in the surf holding the rope, and Gordon Smith's sturdy figure a few paces behind him ready to haul at the signal.

'I don't know what they are confused about, Gordon,' said George impatiently. 'I reckon they're either fools or drunk.'

'They're foreigners I'm thinking,' replied Gordon, 'and don't know what to do with the rope - Frenchmen are right foolish creatures.'

'Oh man but they're signalling haul.'

'No, Gordon, they cannot have fastened the block yet.'

Peering through the darkness these two men tried to discern the movements of the crew, and neither could see any sign of intelligent purpose. Still the lantern dipped, and now as if held by a hasty hand in spasmodic jerks that seemed to say, 'Hasten for the love of God'.

'Pull the rope Geordie and see if anybody is holding it.'

'George cautiously did as Gordon desired, and, feeling a weight, he signalled to haul. All at once he seemed to stagger and shiver, then called out, 'Stop men stop, there is something wrong.'

'What's the matter, Geordie?'

'Come here Gordon, for God's sake.'

Gordon waded up to his companion, who said in awestruck voice, 'Something struck me just now, Gordon, and then wrapped around my leg. Put down your hand and see what it is. I dare not do it, I'm very scared.'

Gordon put down his hand in silence, then started as if he had been stung. His face was working with strong emotion as he looked up to George Milne, and the faint light of early dawn fell on his strong rugged features.

'What's the matter, Gordon man? Can you not tell me?'

'It's a dead man Geordie; his two arms are around your leg.'

Gordon's heart was big and tender, and the tears ran over his cheeks as, lifting the dead man gently, he said, 'Drowned like a rat in a trap poor chap, and him but a young fellow.'

Then he rose to his full height, and, with clenched fist shaken towards the vessel he relieved his feelings in a burst of indignation that did honour to his nature.

Little did he and his companions know that, at the other end of that fatal line, four men were tied by the waist even as this one was. Four men struggling, gasping, fighting with death, tossed among the wreckage of their own ship. Yet so it was, for in the wild frenzy of the time and in gross ignorance of the means of safety, four of the crew had been tied on the line as soon as the first was hauled away. The Captain tied his own son into it, but on his cries for help he had again been hauled aboard, dozed with brandy, and put in the cabin half drowned. George Milne and Gordon Smith carried the dead man ashore, and, as they laid their burden gently on the sands amid the pitiful ejaculations of the crowd, George said, 'it's useless this work: they don't know what they are doing: we must get the lifeboat in position. I don't know what has become of Duthie.'

Most of Duthie's crew had run to the sands, and he had hard work to get volunteers, but now he was seen in the grey light carefully steering his craft towards the wreck. On board the ship the excitement was intense, and it was increased as the lifeboat approached. Two of their mates had been hauled aboard again and laid on deck, but on sight of the lifeboat the other two were forgotten. Ten men stood ready to spring into the boat as soon as she came near. Warning cries arose from Duthie and his crew, when they saw their intention, but the cries fell on deaf ears, and the ten sprang simultaneously into the boat, nearly capsizing her in their mad rush. A perfect babble of shouts and curses in a rough French patois rang out on the night winds as they staggered about impeding the men who would save them. One man persisted in thwarting the efforts of one of the crew who was fending the boat, and he was rendered quiet by a blow that stretched him in the bottom. The boat sheered off safely and landed them all on the sands. The Captain evidently expected to meet his three mates alive and well, and when he saw only one dead man he ran to the life line, held up two fingers, pointed to the ship, and made as if he would haul the line.

The men hauled with a will, and soon two dark forms appeared in the surf - the bodies of two drowned men. With pitiful cries the rescued men threw themselves on the bodies, eagerly placing their hands over their hearts, seeking for signs of life. Less attention a little earlier would have saved their lives. Then Duthie shouted from the lifeboat, 'Are you all there? Ask the Captain if there is any more on the wreck.'

With signs the Captain was made aware of Duthie's question, and he gave a start when he comprehended. He had forgotten his own boy in the cabin. He held up three fingers, and urged them off to the ship. On board they found two men lying on deck, one dead, one with faint signs of life. In the cabin the Captain's boy lay unconscious.

They brought them ashore, and on the bare sand hills they tried to restore animation to the one who showed signs of life, but it was all in vain. Thus a ghastly roll call of five dead men was the result of stupidity, ignorance, and frenzy. These five were laid in the little village hall, and the Captain's boy found a warm bed and effectual nursing from a kind-hearted fisherman's wife.

The Rocket House on the left where the Board of Trade Life Saving Apparatus was stored.

## A LADY BOUNTIFUL (ORIGINAL)

It was now needful to understand the Captain; none knew the language, and he had not a word of English. 'Send up to the Castle for Louise,' said one. Louise was Lady Erroll's maid, and spoke French.

'The Lady will not let Louise come without her breakfast, but she will come herself.' And, sure enough, her Ladyship appeared, and wrought among these foreign fishermen from morning till noon without her breakfast. The Frenchmen were billeted throughout the village in the fishermen's houses.

In a short time the messenger returned, saying Lady Erroll got their names and wrote to their friends. She got the names of the dead men and wrote kind comforting letters to their mothers and wives. She wrote to the authorities, arranged for the burial, and, like a Lady Bountiful, provided meat pies each day for dinner to the survivors so long as they lodged in the Ward. It was a lesson in pure religion and undefiled, in charity that suffereth long and is kind.

These men were all Roman Catholics, and, with thoughtful care, she sent for the Priest at Peterhead for the funeral. It was a sad sight in the little schoolroom with its bare whitewashed walls to see these fine men - three of them young strong fellows, and one old man with his little son, a lad of about fifteen years. The silent and calm dignity of death, which ever rubs out the deep lines of care and riotous passion, appealed to one's deepest emotion, and the thought of widows and orphans weeping unavailing tears far away in Dunkirk made one's eyes well over in sympathy.

There was a hush as of death as the priest pattered over the prayers of his Church, and sprinkled Holy water on the bodies right and left of him, and a stolid satisfaction on the faces of the ten rough Frenchmen as they gazed on the representative of their Church performing the last sad rites over the dead bodies of their comrades.

A thing happened that day which perhaps never happened before in this land. At the hour of burial the Parish Minister and the Congregational Minister stood amid the little crowd of villagers assembled. The hour passed, and no priest appeared. No one seemed to know of any distinct arrangement, and the two Ministers proceeded with the service. In the little crowded Hall the simple Protestant service began, but, before the prayer was ended, Lady Erroll entered accompanied by the priest who had been delayed. At the conclusion of the prayer the Roman Catholic service began, and thus over the bodies of these five strangers three Churches, widely asunder in several ways, united in prayer for common mercies. A service took place next day which stirred the hearts of those who heard it. In a fisherman's kitchen sat ten Frenchmen, smoking and talking together. The door opened, and a lady appeared and entered the cloud of tobacco smoke. The men rose to their feet, and bared their heads. Well they knew her as their Lady Bountiful during these trying days.

'I am glad, gentlemen, that I have found you all together, for I want to speak with you,' she said in French.

The Captain bowed and acknowledged her kindness.

'Don't you think, Captain, that we ought to thank God who has cared for you and saved you from death?'

'Yes Madam, replied the Captain.

'Then let us pray together?' And then, in the midst of that group of French fishermen, our Lady of the sacred heart prayed with them and for them in their own tongue. All was forgotten that separates: the wide gap of difference in social status: the impassable gulf of creed distinction: the subtle difference of sex, and the harder line drawn between alien races - all was forgotten in the calm grace of a Gentlewoman's quiet trust in God.

Weeks after, the Lady read a letter to the minister as they sat in her boudoir at the Castle. It was from the Curè of Dunkirk, and ran as follows:

'My Lady,

In the name of my poor children who were cast on your rocky coast and were succoured by you in their need, I thank you. In the name of the mothers and widows who mourn their dead, and of the wives who in the name rejoice in their husbands, I bless you. In the name of the Blessed Saviour who put it into your heart to cherish the strangers in a strange land, and of the Holy Mother Church, I pray for you, that such a good kind heart as yours may be speedily brought back to the true Fold, and that I may call you truly a sister in Christ, as I am proud to do in charity. May the blessing of them that are ready to perish fall on you my Lady, and on your illustrious house now and ever.'

As she finished, she looked up at the minister with a smile saying, 'The dear good man: he evidently thinks we are all astray. After all, we want to get into the true fold don't we.'

Slains Castle.

## "DUTHIE" (ORIGINAL)

Some men impress you at first sight as men of character. Duthie is one of that sort. His tee name is 'Elikie', but I never heard anyone calling him by his tee name. Usually he is designated Duthie, but, from the first, I called him Mr Duthie. There was a subtle power in the man that commanded respect, and that power did not emanate from his clothes, his education, or his income. I do not suppose that Duthie could boast of £15 annual income: his education was as meagre as his salary, and his clothing suited the man and his work; but he had a good estate in certain real property which we must call manhood. He was a man little of stature, gifted with Lord Byron's mark of a gentleman, little hands and feet; a sturdy trunk and neck wherein good blood was made and plenty of it, which was not wasted on expansive territory.

He stood upright under his weight of three-score years. From heel to crown he was straight as an arrow, and his head was bald save for a fringe of thin hair encircling it like the tonsure of a monk. His face was tanned, seamed, and wrinkled, clean-shaved on Saturday, and stubbly mid-week. A fringe of ragged, grizzled whisker ran down his cheeks and met under his chin. His nose was one that knew things, and his eyes were eyes that laughed at them. His mouth was large, with fine thin lips - the mouth of an orator, filled with teeth strong enough to clip a fishing line. His head was a good one, with a grand swelling dome whose architectural outline was clear cut. There was a fine bump of reverence in it, but withal he was logical and always wanted to know the 'rizzon o' things' and trace them to their consequents. I am careful over his portrait, for I like him. He and the minister did not always agree, but they were always good friends.

He used to say, 'I hae nae chance wi' ye fan it comes

to rizzonin' oot a subject, but a'm no jist agreein' wi' ye, ye'r owre Arminian for me.'

To which the minister would reply, 'Ah Duthie, have you not discovered yet that the Bible is both Arminian and Calvanistic?'

If you desire to see Duthie on his native heath, go down to the Ward Kirk on a Saturday afternoon, and, if the day be fine, you will see the man I have described laying out cushions in the sun over the front railings. He will tell you, 'I'm jist giein' her a bit dicht oot afore the morn.'

His active duty lies between the Church and the Lifeboat of which he is Coxwain, with occasional work at net mending, for his fishing days are over. Duthie has a history, and I commit no breach of confidence when I tell you that he did not always count it an honour to be a doorkeeper in the house of God. He used to be a rough and ready blade, and Peterhead had more attractions for him then, than now. Once he returned from Peterhead by the cliff road, and, overcome by drink and fatigue, he lay down to rest among the whins.

He fell asleep, and thus he describes his waking, 'Fan I cam to mysel' it was pitch dark, an' the win' was soochin' amo' the rocks, an' frestlin' amo' the driet peas o' the whuns far a' was lyin'. I lay on my breist, my tae han' aneath me was sleepin', an' my tither lyin' jist ayont my heid didna touch naething frae aboot my elbow to my fingers.

My chin restet on a bit tourock o' gerse, but frae my mou' up to the croon o' my heid I fan' the waft o' the win', and fat a' thocht was rain. But the thing that fleggit me was a soun at wasna win', fur it roart awa fun the win' gied owre. It cam up frae aneath me, an' fyles a thocht it leuch, an' syne it sabbit wi' a skreich at antern times, an' a rattlin' o' steens. I kent the soun, but I couldna tell far I had heard it, fur my heid was jumblet kin' wi' the fusky I had drunken.

Than a' at ance I brak into a cauld sweat, as pitten oot my han' I fan naithing aneath, an' a blab o' sea suds brak on my face. I was lyin on the edge o' the cliff, wi' my heid half owre, an' the soun I heard was the breakin' o' the waves at the fit. 1 raze on my hands and knees, turned roon an' crawl't back to the fell dyke. Then I up and ran as far frae the sea as I could, an' I didna stop till I was half wyes, at Cruden Manse. That was the last o' ma drinkin'. Thinks I, I may mak a feel man o' masel itherwyes, but fusky'l never get another chance.'

## "DUTHIE" (ENGLISH)

Some men impress you at first sight as men of character. Duthie is one of that sort. His tee name is 'Elikie', but I never heard anyone calling him by his tee name. Usually he is designated Duthie, but, from the first, I called him Mr. Duthie. There was a subtle power in the man that commanded respect, and that power did not emanate from his clothes, his education, or his income. I do not suppose that Duthie could boast of £15 annual income: his education was as meagre as his salary, and his clothing suited the man and his work; but he had a good estate in certain real property which we must call manhood. He was a man little of stature, gifted with Lord Byron's mark of a gentleman, - little hands and feet; a sturdy trunk and neck wherein good blood was made and plenty of it, which was not wasted on expansive territory.

He stood upright under his weight of three-score years. From heel to crown he was straight as an arrow, and his head was bald save for a fringe of thin hair encircling it like the tonsure of a monk. His face was tanned, seamed, and wrinkled, clean-shaved on Saturday, and stubbly mid-week. A fringe of ragged, grizzled whisker ran down his cheeks and met under his chin. His nose was one that knew things, and his eyes were eyes that laughed at them. His mouth was large, with fine thin lips - the mouth of an orator, filled with teeth strong enough to clip a fishing line. His head was a good one, with a grand swelling dome whose architectural outline was clear cut. There was a fine bump of reverence in it, but withal he was logical and always wanted to know the 'reason of things' and trace them to their consequents. I am careful over his portrait, for I like him. He and the Minister did not always agree, but they were always good friends.

He used to say, 'I have no chance with you when it comes

to reasoning out a subject, but I'm not just agreeing with you, you are over Arminian for me.'

To which the minister would reply, 'Ah Duthie, have you not discovered yet that the Bible is both Arminian and Calvanistic?'

If you desire to see Duthie on his native heath, go down to the Ward Kirk on a Saturday afternoon, and, if the day be fine, you will see the man I have described laying out cushions in the sun over the front railings. He will tell you, 'I'm just giving them a cleaning before the morning.'

His active duty lies between the Church and the Lifeboat of which he is Coxwain, with occasional work at net mending, for his fishing days are over. Duthie has a history, and I commit no breach of confidence when I tell you that he did not always count it an honour to be a doorkeeper in the house of God. He used to be a rough and ready blade, and Peterhead had more attractions for him then, than now. Once he returned from Peterhead by the cliff road, and, overcome by drink and fatigue, he lay down to rest among the gorse bushes.

He fell asleep, and thus he describes his waking, 'When I woke up it was pitch dark, and the wind was blowing amongst the rocks, and rustling the dried seed pods of the gorse bushes where I was lying. I lay on my front, one of my two hands lay beneath me and was numb, and my other lying just beyond my head didn't touch anything from about my elbow to my fingers.

My chin rested on a tussock of gorse, but from my mouth up to the crown of my head I felt the draught of the wind, and what I thought was rain. But the thing that scared me was a sound that wasn't wind, because it roared away when the wind went over. It came up from beneath me, and while I thought it laughed, and then it sobbed with a screech at other times, and a rattling of stones. I knew the sound, but I couldn't tell where I had heard it, because my head was pretty jumbled with the whisky I'd drunk.

Then all at once I broke into a cold sweat, as putting out my hand I felt nothing beneath, and a blob of sea foam landed on my face. I was lying on the edge of the cliff, with my head half over, and the sound I heard was the breaking of the waves at the foot. 1 rose on my hands and knees, turned round and crawled back to the turf wall, then I upped and ran as far from the sea as I could, and I didn't stop till I was half way, at Cruden Manse. That was the last of my drinking. Thinks I, I may make a fool of myself otherwise, but whisky will never get another chance.'

# HIS LORDSHIP (ORIGINAL)

It was during these rough, roystering days that Duthie fell out with the Earl. There was little game on the estate, but rabbits ran and burrowed in thousands among the bent-crowned sand hills near the sea. The Earl wanted to preserve his rabbits, and Duthie wanted a share: hence the strife. Duthie had the advantage, as he knew every link of the sand hills by day or night, and the rabbit runs were as plain to him as the village pavements, and about as wide. The gamekeeper had no chance with Duthie, but the Earl was sure that he could catch him.

Div ye ken yon big rock knowe on the fitroad to Hawklaw? said Duthie, in relating this exploit. 'Yon's a gran' place for rabbits, and a braw place fan the meen shines. Well, ae nicht a gyangs oot, jist afore the darknin', alang the san's makin' as a was gyan to Finnyfaulds. Fan I gat to the hard san's I sees a fitstep afore me an' a curran little wee dots alangside o' the fitsteps. Thinks I, that's a man wi' a walkin' stick, and, as nane o' the Ward men ase a walkin' stick, a wunnert fat stranger sud be gyan oot sae late on the san's. I quickent ma step till I gat sicht o' a man jist turnin' in by the edge o' the Hawklaw Burn, and I kent by the cock o' his cap and the set o's back at it was the Yerl. I joukit in by the cleft o' the san' hills far the Blady Burn rins doon, and, fan I gat to the fit o' the rabbit knowe, there was the Yerl at the top o't. He ne'er saw me, as he was lookin frae him oot to the sea, wi' his back to me, so I jist sat doon at the fit quaet kin' and got oot my girns an' pins.

Afore he turned roun a gat twa or three set in the runs, aye keepin' ma ee on him, an' fan he turn't I slippit roun' the knowe as quaet as pussy. I set a dizzen girns that nicht, him stanin' lookin' fur me. He never jaloust onything fur ye see he thocht I wasna forit yet. Efter a while he gantet lood, an' then I heard him steppin' doon to the san's on the road hame, an' a waitet till the mornin'. Neist day I met him in the village and gied him his time o' day, but he jist turnet his back on me and said "Gurrhh", an' spak nane. Somebody had been tellin' him aboot me.

What made me gie up rabbit snarin? Huh! Ye may ken it was naether him nor his gamie that made me dae't. Na na, it was the Leddy did that - a couldna haud oot against her wye o't. Her an' me are great friens. Twa days efter that nicht she wrote a letter and sent it doon wi' Soople Sandy to be pitten in my ain han's.

This was the writin' on't:

"Dear Duthie,

I am so sorry today: Lordship is so angry with you. He believes that you take rabbits on the bents. If it is true, for my sake, dear Duthie, don't do it again - it makes us so miserable."

I couldna stan' that ye ken, so I jist gied it up for the sake o' the Leddy. She his a great respec' for me. A' the polis and gamies in Aberdeen wadna' a made me gie up, but fan a kent at the Leddy was hurtit wi' my ongauns, I didna care tho' a sud never prie a rabbit again.'

'Did the Earl ever change towards you after that?' enquired the minister.

'Oh fye aye, a never gat a soor look frae him efter the Kirk was bigget an' we were a workin' awa thegither. He gruppit me ance getherin' limpits aneath the Castle far he had gien orders we sudna gyang. I was thrang getherin' fan a heard a man rarin' at me to come up oot o' that, an' lookin' up then I saw him shakkin' his stick at me wi's face as reed as a bil't labster.

I jist gethert twa or three mair to let him see at a wasna fleggit, for I kent fine he hadna seen it was me. Then I up till him, an' fan he saw my face he jist leuch an' said, "Oh it's you Duthie I thought it was that fellow Toher who loafs about here.'

I touched my cap, an' says I, "My Lord, gin ye objec' to me comin' here for limpets a winna seek to come; a can han' ther anes in tae the cook as I gyang by the Castle."

"Hold your nonsense, Duthie," he said. "You know well that I don't forbid you - you are one of ourselves you know."

That's the wye o' them a' an' there's a wye o' workin' them. The'l mak ye ane o' themsel's, but the'l no lat you do it. Ye maun naether be upsettin' wi' them nor frichtit for them, an' aye gie them the first place athoot latten them see at ye'r doin' sic like.

Do ye min' yon day fan me an' you was oot wi' Lady Mab at the fishing?'

'I remember that well, and there was a mystery about that fishing I never could understand.'

'Nae doot, nae doot,' replied Duthie smiling. 'Gin ye like a can tell the mystery an' I can explain't tae. Ye was wunnerin' fat wye Lady Mab gruppit a' the big fish an' you got little anes. It was maybe no very pleasant for you, but it was a' wisely order't. Ye see it wad never do to lat Lady Mab be licket at the fishin' even by the minister, an' it wad been waur to lat her see at ony ane was helpin' her. She's a fine lassie, but she's jist like oorsels - its aye a gran' fishin' fan she gets the big anes. Fu did a manage' t? I jist pickit the best bit o' the partans for her heuks, an' gied you fat was left.'

'Oh, that was too bad of you Duthie,' cried the minister.

'Aye that's fat you think, but it was a fur yer gweed. I wantit her to think weel o' the minister, an' a kent she did that fan she lat ye grup her han' to help her oot o' the boat an' owre the rocks an' tangle.

Ye min' she wantit oot some suddent fan the swal cam on. They'r jist like ither fouk at sic times. A heap o' fouk respec' ye as lang's they hae the better o' ye, an' that's the wye o' big fouk.

No that I can speak sic like about oor Castle fouk, but amo' big fouk keep min' at the win's aye kittle to blaw ae airt.'

'I'm sure you never found anything like that about Lady Erann. I hear you visited her when you were in London.'

Oh fie no, she's no that kin' ava: she's a leddy. They new servants at the Castle are far bigger gentry than the Leddy.'

Slains Castle on the horizon; the Kilmarnock Arms Hotel is in the foreground.

## HIS LORDSHIP (ENGLISH)

It was during these rough, roistering days that Duthie fell out with the earl. There was little game on the estate, but rabbits ran and burrowed in thousands among the bent-crowned sand hills near the sea. The earl wanted to preserve his rabbits, and Duthie wanted a share: hence the strife. Duthie had the advantage, as he knew every link of the sand hills by day or night, and the rabbit runs were as plain to him as the village pavements, and about as wide. The gamekeeper had no chance with Duthie, but the earl was sure that he could catch him.

'Do you know that big rock knoll on the foot road to Hawklaw?' said Duthie, in relating this exploit. 'That's a great place for rabbits, and a beautiful place when the moon shines. Well, one night I went out, just before it got dark, along the sands making out I was going to Whinnyfold. When I got to the hard sands I saw a footprint in front of me and some small dots alongside them. Thinks I, that's a man with a walking stick, and, as none of the Ward men use a walking stick, I wondered what stranger would be going out so late on the sands. I quickened my step until I got sight of a man just turning in by the edge of the Hawklaw Burn, and I knew by the cock of his cap and the set of his back that it was the earl. I ducked in by the cleft of the sand hills where the Bleedy Burn runs down, and, when I got to the foot of the rabbit knoll, there was the earl at the top of it. He never saw me, as he was looking out to the sea, with his back to me, so I just sat down at the foot quiet kind and got out my snares and pins.

Before he turned round I got two or three set in the runs, always keeping my eye on him, and when he turned I slipped round the knoll as quiet as a pussy. I set a dozen snares that night, him standing looking for me. He never suspected anything because you see he thought I wasn't ahead of him yet.

After a while he yawned loudly, and then I heard him stepping down to the sands on the road home, and I waited until the morning. Next day I met him in the village and gave him his time of day, but he just turned his back on me and said 'Gurrhh', and said nothing. Somebody had been telling him about me.

What made me give up rabbit snaring? Huh! You may know it was neither him nor his gamekeeper that made me do it. No, no, it was the Lady did that - I couldn't hold out against her way of it. Her and me are great friends. Two days after that night she wrote a letter and sent it down with Supple Sandy to be given to me [Supple Sandy was a servant at Slains Castle who did odd jobs for the Earl and his family. Bram Stoker renamed him as Saft Tammie for his short story *Crooken Sands*].

This was the writing on it:

"Dear Duthie,
I am so sorry today: Lordship is so angry with you. He believes that you take rabbits on the bents. If it is true, for my sake, dear Duthie, don't do it again - it makes us so miserable."

I couldn't stand that you know, so I just gave it up for the sake of the Lady. She has a great respect for me. And the police and the gamekeepers in Aberdeen would not have made me give up, but when I knew that the Lady was upset at my activities, I didn't care whether I should ever take a rabbit again.'

'Did the earl ever change towards you after that?' enquired the minister.

'Oh why yes, I never got a sour look from him after the church was built and we were all working together. He caught me once gathering limpets beneath the Castle where he had given orders we shouldn't go. I was gathering many of them when I heard a man roaring at me to come up out of that, and looking up then I saw him shaking his stick at me with his face as red as a boiled lobster.

I just gathered two or three more to let him see that I wasn't scared, for I knew well he hadn't seen it was me. Then I went up to him, and when he saw my face he just laughed and said, "Oh it's you Duthie I thought it was that fellow Toher who loafs about here."

I touched my cap, and says I, "My Lord, should you object to me coming here for limpets I won't come; I can hand these ones to the cook as I go past the Castle."

"Hold your nonsense, Duthie," he said. "You know well that I don't forbid you - you are one of ourselves you know."

That's the way of them all and there's a way of working them. They will make out you are one of themselves, but will not let you do it. You must neither be upsetting them nor frightened by them, and always give them deference without letting them see that you are doing it.

Do you remember the day when you and me went out with Lady Mab [Lady Erroll] at the fishing?

'I remember that well, and there was a mystery about that fishing I never could understand.'

'No doubt, no doubt,' replied Duthie smiling. 'If you like I can explain the mystery to you. You was wondering why Lady Mab caught all the big fish and you got little ones. It was maybe not very pleasant for you, but it was all sneakily set up. You see it would never do to let Lady Mab be beaten at the fishing even by the minister, and it would not have been right to let her see that anyone was helping her. She's a fine lassie, but she's just like ourselves – it's always great fishing when she gets the big ones. How did I manage it? I just picked the best bit of the small crabs for her hooks, and gave you what was left.'

'Oh, that was too bad of you Duthie,' cried the minister.

'Aye that's what you think, but it was all for your own good. I wanted her to think well of the minister, and I knew she did that when she let you grip her hand to help her out of the boat and over the rocks and seaweed.

You remember she wanted out all of a sudden when the swell came on. They are just like other folk at such times. A lot of people respect you as long as they have the better of you, and that's the way of big folk. Not that I can speak like that about our Castle folk, but amongst big folk, always keep in mind the direction the wind is blowing.

'I'm sure you never found anything like that about Lady Erroll. I hear you visited her when you were in London.'

'Oh why no, she's not that kind at all: she's a lady. Those new servants at the Castle behave more like stuck up gentry than does the Lady.'

[Bram Stoker also mentions the rabbits on the dunes, although they had vanished by the time the golf course opened in 1899. Here are his two comments on the rabbits from before and after the course was built:

'the deep bay, backed with a multitude of bent-grown dunes where the rabbits are to be found in thousands'. *Crooken Sands* (1894).

'I followed the devious sheep track amongst the dunes covered with wet bent-grass, every now and again stumbling amongst the rabbit burrows which in those days honeycombed the sandhills of Cruden Bay.' *The Mystery of The Sea* (1902).

If rabbits inhabit the sand dunes today, I've never seen any.]

# HER LADYSHIP (ORIGINAL)

Na! I enjoyed mysel' weel in London. Ye ken 1 was sent up as a witness in the Fishery Commission. She said a be to come and see her gin a was in London, sae, efter ma work was bye, a jist left the gran' hotel far a was bidin' an' sat out for Kew Cottage. A man telt me far aboot Kew Gairdens war an' fan I cam up to them a sees a young nobleman comin' alang the pavement. Says I till him, 'Can ye tell me, Sir, far Leddy Erann bides?'

He glourt at me, misdootin' me to be a gey roch customer to be speerin' for the likes o' her. Than he spak: 'What do you want with Lady Erann's house? Do you know her?'

'I day ken Lady Erann,' says I, 'An' I'll fin't oot for masel' gin ye dinna pint it oot.'

Wi' that I steppit oot, but I hadna gaen far afore I heard quick steps ahint me. I never jeet ma heid, but fan he cam up to me he tiched me on the shoother an' says he, 'I beg your pardon: I was not quite sure, but since you know Lady Erann I will show you her house. See, it's that house past two openings on the left.'

'Thenk ye Sir,' says I, 'Ye needna be feart. I dinna only ken her, but am here on her ain inveet, but a'l no tell on ye.' He leuch and took a reed face, an' I gaed up to the door an' rang the bell.

Henderson, the butler, opened it, an' at sicht o' me jist held up baith's han's and said, 'Bless me, Duthie, is this you? Come away in: her Ladyship has company, but she will be glad to see you.'

Weel a wat she was gled. She had a lot o' Lords an' Ladies an' sic like at their lunch, but she couldna hae ta' en muckle mair time than jist to dicht her mou' afore she was doon at me an' gruppit me by baith han's an' said, 'Dear Duthie, this is delightful to see your face again,' an' she set me doon on a sofa by hersel' an' spak kin' an' fan I could look at her she was weepin'. Syne she speert for Kirsty an' Jeanie an' Sandy an' the auld Pilot, an' a' the fouk aboot the Ward. Than she raze an' rang the bell sayin', 'Oh this is pleasant Duthie, but I am selfish not offering you anything to eat.'

Henderson cam' to the door, and my Leddy said, 'Bring something for Duthie to eat.'

Syne fan he brocht me as gweed a dinner as ane could wish for, she said, 'Now Duthie I will leave you and Henderson together till my company leaves.'

Aboot tea time she cam' back to the room an' we sat an' talket aboot the Ward, an' auld times, an' his Lordship, an' the Kirk, an' than she said, 'Now Duthie, you and I are going to have tea together; I want a long talk with you yet.'

'Oh my Leddy,' I said, 'I canna tak' ma tea wi' you, it's no for the likes o' me to be sittin' at the same table wi' you.'

'Don't say that Duthie,' she said. 'You and I have sat at the Lord's table together, and surely you will not refuse me this pleasure. In a few years what is left of you and me will not show much difference.'

Efter we had oor tea an' had talket a lang while I raze an' said, 'I maun be gyan awa back to ma ludgins my Leddy, afore it's dark.'

'No Duthie,' she said. 'You are not to do that, you must stay with us tonight; you must indeed.'

'Na ma Leddy,' said I, 'it's vera kin' o' ye, an' I'm prood o' it, but I canna stay in your hoose a' nicht.'

'Duthie,' says she, 'Go away to Henderson's room and smoke with him, and we'll speak about this afterwards.'

Was't no wunnerfu fu' she kent a was needin' a smoke. That's aye the wye o' her. She watches ye like a hawk to see if yer missin' onything, an' tries to mak up for't.

Weel she wadna hear o' me gyan. 'Duthie,' says she, 'do you agree with the rule of the majority?'

'I maun dae that my Leddy,' says I, 'There's naethin' else for't.'

'Please to ring the bell Henderson,' says she. Than the door open't an' a' the servants cam' in lauchin'.

'Duthie has agreed to abide by the vote of the majority,' says my Leddy. 'Hands up those who want him to stay here tonight.'

Wi' that she held up her ain han' an' they a' did the same. 'Now Duthie,' she said, 'If you want inducement, see I'll make up a bed for you myself.'

Could ony man stan' the like o' that? I jist leuch an' said I wad bide.

An' that was the Leddy at made ma bed for me in London, an' a safter I never lay on. I didna' need to rise an' shift the lumps o't, or dig my elbows in't to get peace to sleep. Fan I lay doon it raze up in rowes aboot me like to smoor me. The bed an' me was jist on a level jist as if I had been planed doon to fit it.

Aye, but I sleepit fine, an' could har'ly think to come oot o't in the mornin'. I was that warm an' cozy kin', an' sleepy an' weel pleas't wi' a' thing, a wad jist a lain still. But a chap cam' to the door, an' a servant said it was half nine an' she had set my sheen an' het water at the door. Up I got an' keekit oot at the door. There war my sheen glitterin' new brushed, an' aside them a little wee reed rooser wi' het water.

Says I to mysel', 'This is ane o' their gentry wyes na, but I kenna fat the het watter's fur. Fan yer eatin' wi them it's a kittle coorse to steer amo' the twa three pair knives an' forks an' speens at they set afore ye, but ye can aye watch yer neist neebor. Am a' ma lane here an' a maun let them see at a ken gentry wyes. Lat's see. They wash their han's an' face ilka mornin', but there's cauld watter in the pitcher fur that. It's owre muckle fur shavin', an' it canna be fur drinkin. Surely they canna wash their feet ilka mornin?'

I was fair jumblet, but than I thocht, they needna ken fu' I aset it, so I'll jist wash ma han's an face in't, and that'l lat them see at I'm no ohn kennan gentle folks wyes. I pat some cauld watter amo' the het to mak' it loo kin', an' it was gran'. Aye sin' syne I gar Jeanie gie me loo watter fan the biler's gaun in the mornin.

Efter breakfast my Leddy took me oot a walk through the gairdens, an' mony a body lookit at us, wunnerin' fat oora man she had taen up wi, but she never mismaid hersel', an' a enjoyed mysel' weel.

Fan I was comin' awa she sent for a conveyance to tak me to the station an' made up a piece for me to eat on the road. Than she gied me that velvet purse ye see hingin' on the wa', fu' o' cut tobacco, an' a wudden pipe in a case. Leddy Mab stappit a pock o' shag in ma pooch as big as that for auld Sandy. I didna open ma piece till I was ayont Aberdeen, for I canna eat in the train. I offert it to twa mason chaps in the carriage, an' they lookit queer kin' at me.

'Ye needna look,' says I, 'It's nae lauchin'. Div ye ken fa made up that piece for me? That piece was made up by the Right Honourable the Countess of Erann, sae ye may think muckle o' the offer.'

Wi that they took it, an' fan they pried it they said they never had a piece like that. It was little wee thin shaves o' breed, twa laid thegither, an', atween the twa, slices o' ham an' chicken an' mustard at jist meltet in the mou' an' made ye wish for anither.

Oh sir, she's a Leddy, she's a Leddy: gin there was mair a' her kin' in the warld, peer fouk wad never say at gentle fouk war prood.

# HER LADYSHIP (ENGLISH)

No! I enjoyed myself well in London. You know, 1 was sent up as a witness in the Fishery Commission. She said I should come and see her if I was in London, so after my work was done, I left the grand hotel where I was staying and set out for Kew Cottage. A man told me where to find Kew Gardens and when I came up to them I saw a young nobleman coming along the pavement. Says I to him, 'Can you tell me, sir, where Lady Erroll stays?'

He glowered at me, sizing me up as a rough customer to be asking for the likes of her. Then he spoke: 'What do you want with Lady Erroll's house? Do you know her?'

'I do know Lady Erroll,' says I, 'And I'll find out for myself if you don't point her house out.'

With that I stepped out, but I hadn't gone far before I heard quick steps behind me. I never turned my head, but when he came up to me he touched me on the shoulder and says he, 'I beg your pardon: I was not quite sure, but since you know Lady Erroll I will show you her house. See, it's that house past two openings on the left.'

'Thank you sir,' says I, 'You need not be afraid. Not only do I know her, I am here at her invitation, but I will not tell on you.' He laughed and took a red face, and I went up to the door and rang the bell.

Henderson, the butler, opened it, and at the sight of me just held up both hands and said, 'Bless me, Duthie, is this you? Come away in: her Ladyship has company, but she will be glad to see you.'

Well I knew she was glad. She had a lot of Lords and Ladies and such like at their lunch, but she couldn't have taken much more time than it took to clean her mouth before she was down to see me, and gripped me by both hands and said, 'Dear

Duthie, this is delightful to see your face again,' and she set me down on a sofa by herself and spoke, and when I looked at her she was crying. Then she asked for Kirsty and Jeanie and Sandy and the old Pilot, and all the folk about the Ward. Then she rose and rang the bell saying, 'Oh this is pleasant Duthie, but I am selfish in not offering you anything to eat.'

Henderson came to the door, and my Lady said, 'Bring something for Duthie to eat.'

Then when he brought me as good a dinner as one could wish for, she said, 'Now Duthie I will leave you and Henderson together till my company leaves.'

About tea time she came back to the room and we sat and talked about the Ward, and old times, and his Lordship, and the Church, and then she said, 'Now Duthie, you and I are going to have tea together; I want a long talk with you yet.'

'Oh my Lady,' I said, 'I cannot take my tea with you, it's not for the likes of me to be sitting at the same table with you.'

'Don't say that Duthie,' she said. 'You and I have sat at the Lord's table together, and surely you will not refuse me this pleasure. In a few years what is left of you and me will not show much difference.'

After we had our tea and had talked a long while I rose and said, 'I must be going away back to my lodgings my Lady, before it's dark.'

'No Duthie,' she said, 'you are not to do that, you must stay with us tonight; you must indeed.'

'No my Lady,' said I, it's very kind of you and I'm proud of it, but I cannot stay in your house all night.'

'Duthie,' says she, 'Go away to Henderson's room and smoke with him, and we'll speak about this afterwards.'

Was it not wonderful how she knew I was needing a smoke. That's always the way of her. She watches you like a hawk to see if you are missing anything, and tries to make up for it.

Well she wouldn't hear of me going. 'Duthie,' says she, 'do you agree with the rule of the majority?'

'I must do that my Lady,' says I. 'There's nothing else for it.'

'Please to ring the bell Henderson,' says she. Then the door opened and all the servants came in laughing.

'Duthie has agreed to abide by the vote of the majority,' says my Lady, 'Hands up those who want him to stay here tonight.'

With that she held up her hand and they all did the same. 'Now Duthie,' she said, 'If you want inducement, see I'll make up a bed for you myself.'

Could any man stand the like of that? I just laughed and said I would stay.

And that was the Lady that made my bed for me in London, and a softer one I never lay on. I didn't need to rise and shift the lumps out of it, or dig my elbows in it to get peace to sleep. When I lay down it rose up in rows about me as if to smother me. The bed and me was just on a level just as if I had been planed down to fit it.

Aye, but I slept fine, and could hardly think to come out of it in the morning. I was that warm and cosy, and sleepy and well pleased with everything, I would just have lain still. But a chap came to the door, and a servant said it was half nine and she had set my shoes and hot water at the door. Up I got and peeked out of the door. There were my shoes glittering new brushed, and beside them a little wee red jug with hot water.

Says I to myself, 'This is one of their gentry ways, but I don't know what the hot water is for. When you are eating with them it's a tricky course to steer among the two or three pairs of knives and forks and spoons they set before you, but you can always watch your nearest neighbour. I'm on my own here and I must let them see I know gentry ways. Let's see. They wash their hands and face every morning, but there's cold water in the pitcher for that. It's more than required for shaving, and it cannot be for drinking. Surely they cannot wash their feet every morning?'

I was fair perplexed, but then I thought, they need not know how I used it, so I'll just wash my hands and face in it, and that will let them see that I know gentle folks ways. I put some cold water amongst the hot to make it lukewarm, and it was grand.

Ever since then I get Jeanie to give me lukewarm water when the boiler is going in the morning.

After breakfast my Lady took me out for a walk through the gardens, and lots of people looked at us, wondering what odd-job man she had taken up with, but she wasn't at all bothered herself, and I thoroughly enjoyed myself.

When I was coming away she sent for a conveyance to take me to the station and made up a sandwich for me to eat on the road. Then she gave me that velvet purse you see hanging on the wall, full of cut tobacco, and a wooden pipe in a case. Lady Mab stuffed a pouch of shag tobacco in my pocket as big as that for old Sandy. I didn't open my snack until I was the other side of Aberdeen, because I cannot eat in the train. I offered it to two mason chaps in the carriage, and they looked strangely at me.

'You needn't look like that,' says I, 'I'm serious. Do you know who made up that sandwich for me? That sandwich was made up by the Right Honourable the Countess of Erroll, so take the offer seriously.'

With that they took it, and when they tasted it they said they never had a sandwich like that. It was little wee thin shaves of bread, two laid together, and, between the two, slices of ham and chicken and mustard that just melted in the mouth and made you wish for another.

Oh sir, she's a Lady, she's a Lady: if there was more of her kind in the world, poor folk would never say that gentle folk were proud.

# A SOLDIER'S DAUGHTER (ORIGINAL)

Fan she sets her min' on a thing ye maun jist gie in. She's a sodjer's dochter an' the wife o' a sodjer, an' she likes fine to drive fouk specially fur ther gweed. Well I min' that day she rade the white horse o' the Sultan's. But a forget ye didna ken aboot that. It's that horse at she's pentit wi' in the big Dinin' Room o' the Castle.

Did ye no ken she gaed through the Crimean War wi' the Yerl, an' campit oot wi' the rest o' them? Ae day a flag o' truce was to be carriet, an' she did it wi' her ain han' richt up to the Rooshians. Naething' will fleg her fan she sees a thing maun be dune. The Sultan o' Turkey was sae ta'en wi' her at he gied her a fine white Arab horse, an' he was a kittle ane.

Ae day efter she cam' back she rade that horse, an' a finer wumman a never saw on a saiddle. He was kickin' and rearin' an' stannin on's fore feet an' letten flee frae him a' airts, but he couldna cast her, an' she wadna lat the coachman grup his heid. She was white in the face, but her lips were as ticht as a mussel.

She didna strike him, but strokit him on the neck an' said 'Sultan! Sultan!!' that was a'. She wrocht him that wye till she got him to the fit o' the Chapel Hill, than she gied him his wages. Her whup came owre his flank an' he sprang forit like a wullicat an' up the hill full gallop. He wad a stoppit half up, but again the whup cut him an' he didna get stoppin' till she wad let him. Efter that he was aye quaet wi' the Leddy. She widna stop at anything thae days.

Ance the lifeboat wantit a volunteer crew, an' we couldna get naebody to gyang, tho' the ship was breakin' up an' men war like to be lost. Some men wantit to gyang, but the women hung on to them an' wadna lat them. My Leddy cam through the thrang o' them, and a saw by the curl o' her lip an' the flash o' her ee at her bluid was up.

She said, 'You want volunteers, Duthie?'

'Yes my Leddy,' says I.

'Then I am one,' says she. 'Give me your hand Duthie.' An' I helpit her owre the gunnle.

Man ye sud a seen their faces; by the looks o' them a saw they war fair cowet an' remorsin'. It needit jist ae thing an' my Leddy was ready wi't.

Up she gat an' said, 'Men, will you stand there and be shamed by a woman? Come.'

She was like a queen that day. An' they jist cam three-fauld an' pled wi' my Leddy to bide ashore. I weel believe she wad a gane wi' me a' her lane, but I telt her she wad be better to bide an' talk to the women sin' we had plenty o' men. There's mair nor ae Grace Darlin' in the world.

# A SOLDIER'S DAUGHTER (ENGLISH)

When she sets her mind on something you must just give in. She's a soldier's daughter and the wife of a soldier, and she likes fine to drive folk specially for their good. Well I mind that day she rode the white horse of the Sultan's. But I forget you don't know about that. It's that horse she's painted with in the big dining room of the Castle.

Did you not know that she went through the Crimean War with the earl, and camped out with the rest of them? One day a flag of truce was to be carried, and she did it with her own hand right up to the Russians. Nothing will scare her when she sees a thing must be done. The Sultan of Turkey was so taken with her that he gave her a fine white Arab horse, and he was a touchy one.

One day after she came back she rode that horse, and a finer woman I never saw on a saddle. He was kicking and rearing and standing on his forelegs and letting fly all over the place, but he couldn't throw her, and she wouldn't let the coachman grip his head. She was white in the face, but her lips were as tight as a mussel.

She didn't strike him, but stroked him on the neck and said 'Sultan! Sultan!!' that was all. She wrought him that way until she got him to the foot of the Chapel Hill, then she gave him his wages. Her whip came over his flank and he sprang forward like a wildcat and up the hill full gallop. He would have stopped half way up, but again the whip cut him and he didn't get stopping till she would let him. After that he was always quiet with the Lady. She wouldn't stop at anything those days.

Once the lifeboat wanted a volunteer crew, and we couldn't get anybody to go, though the ship was breaking up and men were likely to be lost. Some men wanted to go, but the women hung on to them and wouldn't let them. My Lady came through the crowd of them, and I saw by the curl of her lip and the flash of her eye that her blood was up.

She said, 'You want volunteers, Duthie?'

'Yes my Lady,' says I.

'Then I am one,' says she. 'Give me your hand Duthie.'

And I helped her over the gunwale of the boat.

Man you should have seen their faces; by the looks of them I saw they were pretty cowed and remorseful. It needed just one thing and my Lady was ready with it.

Up she got and said, 'Men, will you stand there and be shamed by a woman? Come.'

She was like a queen that day. And they just came three-fold and pleaded with my Lady to stay ashore. I well believe she would have gone with me on her own, but I told her she would be better to stay and talk to the women since we had plenty of men. There's more than one Grace Darling in the world.

The Countess of Erroll and Sultan (courtesy of Merlin Hay, Earl of Erroll).

## 4. BRAM STOKER AND THE FISHERMEN OF PORT ERROLL

Noel Stoker, who was with his parents on their Port Erroll holidays, told his father's first biographer that 'one of Bram's particular delights was in yarning with the local fishermen' [Harry Ludlam, 2000. *My Quest for Bram Stoker*].

What they talked about is unrecorded. Bram Stoker's diaries and notebooks from the time are missing (as are the Stoker family photographs taken in Port Erroll mentioned by Harry Ludlam: 'Noel showed me albums of holiday snaps but there were none that would reproduce well in my intended book').

It is known that Bram Stoker kept a notebook while in the village. The archive box of material collected by James Drummond contains an unpublished interview with a woman in Cruden Bay who remembered Bram Stoker: 'Mrs Beagrie at the "Red House" liked him, but was disconcerted by his habit of pulling out his notebook in the middle of a conversation and writing things down. But apart from that he was polite.'

The discussion to follow expands on the observation that Bram liked to speak to the local fishermen. It is of necessity speculation on the subject of what they talked about; 'informed speculation' perhaps.

The first proposition is unlikely to be challenged: for Bram to talk to the fishermen he needed to understand their Doric dialect. The dialogue in Adam Drummond's sketches makes it abundantly clear that this would have been a huge challenge for any outsider. Nevertheless, Bram appears to have grasped the Doric dialect relatively quickly because he went on to write dialogue in Doric in his two Cruden Bay set novels, albeit a toned-down version his English readers could cope with. He even slipped a recognisable Doric phrase into *Dracula* which was probably intended as a tribute to the locals - 'I wouldn't fash masel'. The phrase appears twice in *Dracula*, the second time as 'Don't ye fash about them'. Other recognisable Doric words in *Dracula* (scunner, sark) are also known from the Yorkshire dialect, and are found in the reference book Bram Stoker used to write the Yorkshire dialogue spoken by seaman Swales.

Yet, it might be thought surprising that Bram Stoker talked to the fishermen at all, given that he mixed on a daily basis with the elite of London Society. Read these excerpts from the reminiscences of his friend Horace Wyndham and you will see what I mean. They describe one of Bram's responsibilities in his full-time job as the manager of the Lyceum Theatre, the theatre of choice for the London elite:

> To see Stoker in his element was to see him standing at the top of the theatre's stairs, surveying a 'first-night' crowd trooping up them. There was no mistake about it - a Lyceum premiere did draw an audience that really was representative of the best of that period in the realms of art, literature, and society. Admittance was a very jealously guarded privilege. Stoker, indeed, looked upon the stalls, dress circle, and boxes as if they were annexes to the Royal Enclosure at Ascot, and one almost had to be proposed and seconded before the coveted ticket would be issued. The rag-tag-and-bobtail of the musical comedy, theatrical, stock exchange and journalistic worlds who foregather at a present-day premiere would certainly have been sent away with a flea in their ear.

Wyndham also describes how the upper crust of London society flocked to parties at Bram's home:

> The Stokers lived just off the King's Road, Chelsea; and, as they knew everybody worth knowing, and were also exceedingly hospitable, one could always make sure of finding interesting people there. Among those whom I thus met on several occasions was W. S. Gilbert. Sir William,

of course, if only as a librettist of real distinction, had an interesting personality. Candour, however, compels me to remark that it was not an agreeable one. The truth is, he always (as he grew older) conducted himself in a most irascible fashion, and habitually barked at inoffensive strangers like a stage colonel. One afternoon when I happened to be there, a young actress asked Stoker to introduce her to the great man. It was an inopportune moment, for Gilbert, who was in a worse temper than usual - I fancy he must have overheard some tactless person praising Sullivan - shook his head fiercely. 'Don't want to know her,' he growled. 'Want to be left alone.' [Horace Wyndham, 1922. *The Nineteen Hundreds*]

Even though he socialised with the elite, Bram Stoker was open and friendly to everyone without distinction. This appears to have been who he was, although let's also add that he aimed to follow the advice of his spiritual guide, Walt Whitman. Whitman wrote: 'have patience and indulgence toward the people, take off your hat to nothing known or unknown or to any man or number of men, go freely with powerful uneducated persons and with the young and with the mothers of families... [Should you do this] your very flesh shall be a great poem.'

Likewise, Bram Stoker bonded with the fisher folk of Port Erroll. Here he discovered a more authentic and earthy way of life compared to that of the Chelsea dinner party set.

So what did Bram Stoker and the fishermen of Port Erroll talk about? The merest hints are to be found in Bram Stoker's writings.

Take for example, Sandy Summers, a simpleton employed as a servant in the castle. He was known to the locals as Supple Sandy or Sandy Sheep. Adam Drummond refers to him as Soople Sandy; whereas Bram Stoker gave him the fictional name of Saft Tammie in his short story *Crooken Sands* (1894).

A newspaper article about Sandy Summers was published in the *Press and Journal* [March 10, 1923] and displays his photograph: a rather scruffy individual with a far-away look. His fellow servants in the castle liked to play practical jokes on Sandy. For example, one of his daily tasks involved pumping up seawater for the earl's bath every morning. On occasion, he was mightily puzzled that despite his best efforts the bath was still empty – the servants having removed the bath plug when he wasn't watching.

Sandy took his work very seriously. He demanded instant attention at the post office when picking up the castle mail, or when getting groceries at the general stores – informing the counter staff very haughtily that he was the earl's servant and he had a home to go to.

The following extract from *Crooken Sands* is of particular interest. After a lengthy discussion of Sandy's previous history before arriving in the village, the main character of Bram Stoker's story adds:

> The minister who gave the information finished thus:
>
> 'It is a very strange thing, but the man seems to have some odd kind of gift. Whether it be that "second sight" which we Scotch people are so prone to believe in, or some other occult form of knowledge, I know not, but nothing of a disastrous tendency ever occurs in this place but the men with whom he lives are able to quote after the event some saying of his which certainly appears to have foretold it. He gets uneasy or excited – wakes up, in fact – when death is in the air.'

Bram Stoker (courtesy of the Bram Stoker Estate).

We will never know whether Saft Tammie's second sight is a plot device or whether the locals actually believed that Sandy Summers was granted with the gift of the second sight. This is the first mention of second sight in Bram Stoker's writings; a subject he would take much interest in later on. Incidentally, the minister cited above was probably Adam Drummond, and I reckon he would had been annoyed at seeing himself quoted in print about a supernatural subject without also being shown to disapprove of it. Perhaps Bram Stoker made several more tactless mis-steps like this with the minister as time went on.

In Bram's novel *The Mystery of the Sea* set around Port Erroll, his leading character discusses the witch-woman Gormala who hails originally from the Western Isles of Scotland (and speaks in the Doric dialect): 'It was evident that, Christian though she might be - and in the West they are generally devout observants of the duties of their creed - her belief in this respect came from some of the old pagan mythologies.'

Bram Stoker was forever on the lookout for material for his books, and researched local history, folklore, and superstitions to find it. For example, the hundred-year-old smuggling tales still told in the village in his time shaped the plot for *The Watter's Mou'*, and the Spanish shipwreck from the time of the Armada, the remains of which lie on the seabed near Collieston, provides a key plot element in *The Mystery of the Sea*.

But could it be that the ancient superstitions of the Port Erroll fisher folk helped to inspire Bram's supernatural stories including *Dracula*? Such speculation heads towards the wilder shores, although James Drummond believed this to be the case (he once proposed a book to Aberdeen University Press, which, if published, would have integrated Adam Drummond's essays with a discussion of local superstitions tied to Bram Stoker's novels). In James's archive is a copy of Reverend Walter Gregor's book *An Echo of the Olden Time From the North of Scotland*. Walter Gregor, an Aberdeenshire minister who collected local folklore, gleefully recounted supernatural beliefs about death in this book. Indeed the two chapters headed 'Death Omens' and 'Death, and Burial' are as wonderfully ghoulish as anything to be found in *Dracula*.

James Drummond reckoned that Gregor's book influenced Bram Stoker while writing *Dracula*. Yet, I have not found any evidence that Bram read anything by Walter Gregor. Not that I think this matters because Bram would have discovered much of what is described in Gregor's book at first hand on talking to the fisher folk of Port Erroll himself.

It is curious to note that James Drummond's grandfather, the minister, only fleetingly mentions the fisher folk's superstitions in his stories, probably because he didn't approve of them. The history of the Protestant Church in Aberdeenshire since the Reformation in Scotland is a record of how Church ministers relentlessly discouraged their parishioners from believing in witches, fairies, mermaids, and various other supernatural entities; without much success it has to be said.

Yet, Walter Gregor was one of a new breed of Church ministers who in Victorian times took a keen interest in local folklore, traditions, and superstitions - a trend inspired by the work of the

Brothers Grimm in Germany.

Reverend James Rust, the Minister of Slains Parish Church, six miles to the south of Cruden Bay, was another man of the cloth who took an interest in local folklore. Some of his thoughts are written up in his wonderfully-titled and rather eccentric book *Druidism Exhumed* (1871). Here is to be found some curious ideas about the local area; ideas that would have excited Bram Stoker's interest had he read them. For example, Reverend Rust believed the name Slains to derive from the Gaelic for 'High-Plain of the Sorcery' and that of the nearby farm of Clochtow from the Gaelic for Black Stone, that is, as 'connected with the Black-art of Druidical Sorcery'. Everywhere he looked, Reverend Rust found what he considered to be the relics of Druid Black Magic.

Reverend Adam Drummond mentions only one fishermen's superstition in his stories. In *Why Pegsie's Blind Was Not Drawn* he writes that Pegsie told the minister 'I was eerie kin' thinkin' o' the chaps that come to some fouks at siccan times fan their ain fouk are droonin'.' ['I was eerily thinking of the knocks that come to some people when their own folk are drowning'].

Walter Gregor discusses such eerie knocks at length in his 'Death Omens' chapter from *An Echo of the Olden Time From the North of Scotland*:

> Three knocks were heard at regular intervals of one or two minutes' duration. They might be heard in any part of the dwelling-house, on the entrance door, on a table, on the top of a bun bed. Their sound was quite different from any other. It was dull and heavy, and had something eerie about it. A similar omen was the dead-drap. Its sound resembled that of a continued drop of water falling slowly and regularly from a height, but it was leaden and hollow. Such sounds were heard at any time during night or day. Night, however, was the usual time when they were heard. They were heard first by one, and could not be heard by a second without taking hold of the one that first heard

them. This was the case with all the sights and sounds that prognosticated death, and lasted for any length of time.

James Drummond was fascinated by the following gruesome passage from Walter Gregor's book, believing it to echo the ending of *Dracula*. When Van Helsing's gang closes in on Count Dracula in Transylvania, a grim fight to the death ensues. The outcome: the evil count is dispatched 'and before our very eyes and almost in the drawing of a breath, the whole body crumbled into dust and passed from our sight'.

This is the relevant passage from Reverend Gregor's book - those of faint heart are advised to look away now:

> Peculiar horror was manifested towards suicides. Such were not buried in the churchyard. It is not much over half a century since a fierce fight took place in a churchyard in the middle of Banffshire, to prevent the burial of a suicide in it. By an early hour all the strong men of the parish who were opposed to an act so sacrilegious were astir and hastening to the churchyard with their weapons of defence - strong sticks. The churchyard was taken possession of, and the walls manned. The gate and more accessible parts of the wall were assigned to picked men. In due time the suicide's coffin appeared, surrounded by an excited crowd, for the most part armed with sticks. Some, however, carried spades sharpened on the edge. Fierce and long was the fight at the gate, and not a few rolled in the dust. The assailing party was beaten off.
>
> A grave was dug outside the churchyard, close beneath the wall, and the coffin laid in it. The lid was lifted, and a bottle of vitriol poured over the body. Before the lid could be again closed, the fumes of the dissolving body were rising thickly over the heads of actors and spectators. This was done to prevent the body from being lifted during the coming night from its resting place, conveyed back to its abode when in life, and placed against the door, to fall at the

feet of the member of the family that was the first to open the door in the morning.

Had Bram Stoker read this? Perhaps, perhaps not. Anyway, I reckon the ending of *Dracula* is consistent with the book's basic plot and required no prompting from any source material, Walter Gregor or otherwise. The plot of *Dracula* could be that of a cowboy film: the bad guy rides into town and causes trouble – the good guys form a posse and fight back – and in the final dramatic scene the bad guy is violently done away with. Good riddance...

Nevertheless, Walter Gregor does mention a popular fireside story from Aberdeenshire which could explain why Count Dracula has no shadow:

...how men went to Italy and Spain to study the black airt; how, when studying the hellish art, the students had, on leaving the lecture-room, to rush through a long, black passage where the devil was waiting for the last one, and how one escaped by calling out that there was one behind him, and how the Devil seized his shadow, and the man never cast a shadow afterwards...

This item of folklore is also recorded from the Highlands and Islands of Scotland, and may have been a well-known supernatural tale in Victorian times.

Gregor in a superb piece of prose adds that these fireside stories told in Aberdeenshire were:

for the most part of the supernatural... how men and women sold themselves to Satan in exchange for the occult powers, and how they died in horrible terror, and amidst the war of the elements, and how, when they came to be buried, human strength was at times unavailing to carry the coffin to the grave, and how it had to be dragged by a team of horses amid the raging of the tempest. All such was current; and as tale succeeded tale, and the big peat fire began to fade, the younger members of the family crept nearer and nearer the older ones, and, after a little, seated themselves on their knees, or between them and the fire, with the eyes now fearfully turned to the doors, and now to the chimney, and now to this corner, whence issued the smallest noise, and now to the next, in dread of seeing some of the uncanny brood.

Walter Gregor's books may or may not have provided material for *Dracula*. That aside, I reckon two particular aspects of Bram Stoker's yarning with the Port Erroll fishermen may have helped to influence the mood of the novel.

First, Bram Stoker on encountering the fisher folk of Port Erroll had discovered a community steeped in the supernatural, and in particular, one that believed in superstitions and traditions about death. With his wide reading of folklore, Bram would have recognised these superstitions as pagan (pre-Christian) in origin.

He had come across something similar in Emily Gerard's article on *Transylvanian Superstitions*; a key source which Bram Stoker admitted in a newspaper interview had helped to inspire *Dracula*.

Emily Gerard wrote about the folklore of rural Transylvania - her husband, a cavalry officer, had been posted there. In Transylvania were isolated communities hidebound by hundreds of superstitions of ancient origin. On reading Emily's article you are struck by the similarity of style and subject matter to Walter Gregor's book on the North of Scotland.

This is her introduction:

> Transylvania might well be termed the land of superstition, for nowhere else does this curious crooked plant of delusion flourish as persistently and in such bewildering variety. It would almost seem as though the whole species of demons, pixies, witches, and hobgoblins, driven from the rest of Europe by the wand of science, had taken refuge within this mountain rampart, well aware

that here they would find secure lurking-places, whence they might defy their persecutors yet awhile.

She then expresses the opinion that:

> Many old Pagan ceremonies are still clearly to be distinguished through the flimsy shrouding of a later period, and their origin unmistakable even through the surface-varnish of Christianity which was thought necessary to adapt them to newer circumstances, and like a clumsily remodelled garment the original cut frequently asserts itself, despite the fashionable trimmings which now adorn it.

Here's the bit in Gerard's article that must have excited Bram Stoker:

> ...every person killed by a nosferatu becomes likewise a vampire after death, and will continue to suck the blood of other innocent people till the spirit has been exorcised, either by opening the grave of the person suspected and driving a stake through the corpse, or firing a pistol shot into the coffin. In very obstinate cases it is further recommended to cut off the head and replace it in the coffin with the mouth filled with garlic, or to extract the heart and burn it, strewing the ashes over the grave.

Bram Stoker had never been to Transylvania, and would have had to accept Emily Gerard's account of the place at second hand. Nevertheless, what she described in Transylvania could also have been written about the beliefs of the fisher folk of Port Erroll, minus the vampires and the garlic. Bram had discovered in Aberdeenshire an isolated community where day-to-day life was bounded by superstition, much as Emily Gerard had found in Transylvania: the difference being that in Port Erroll he witnessed this for himself at first hand.

It is relevant to mention my own experiences here. Some time ago I worked in Borneo, and while there, I lived in the heart of a Chinese community. I became immersed in all things Chinese and found my new-found Chinese friends more than happy to talk about their superstitions and traditions. And what I discovered in Borneo is what Emily Gerard found in Transylvania, and Bram Stoker undoubtedly found in Port Erroll – a self-contained community whose day-to-day lives are hidebound and dictated to by hundreds of superstitions, largely ancient in origin, and many of them specific to death. To give an example, hotels in Chinese communities rarely contain a fourth floor because the sound of their word for four is very similar to the word 'to die'. Four is thus an inauspicious number for Chinese people (I heard that word 'inauspicious' a lot while I was out there).

I can thus relate to both Emily Gerard and Bram Stoker. What I discovered fascinated me absolutely. It served to educate me about who I am as a person and what influences this. I pondered about what had been responsible for shaping my formative years, concluding that as an infant you had no prior experience to help make sense of anything because your moonshine detectors had not developed yet. So we all started out by believing everything we were told because we had no way of doing otherwise. Adults were the authority figures in our young lives: everything they said to you is the way it had to be.

So right from the very start our minds are filled up with our parent's attitudes, morals, and standards of behaviour. We are in no position to be critical about any of this yet, and as such they will remain within our heads for a long time - probably for the rest of our lives. Our parents went through the same process, as did their parents before them. And similar to how the genes in our DNA work, society's beliefs and cultural traditions are passed down through the generations, having slowly evolved over time. The world view of many people, some who lived centuries ago, is programmed into our minds. I share the moral code and taboos of the Scottish culture I live in. And because of this, I reckon my daily actions are partially governed by the living thoughts of Jesus Christ, John Calvin, and the inherited collective traditions of my fellow Scots.

You get the drift – it is very difficult to escape the imprint of the culture you live in. This is why it is so fascinating to experience a different culture from your own and to observe how it shapes the outlook of the people in it - an ancient way of life preserved as a living fossil of human behaviour, and as such it is a wonder to behold.

What makes this even more poignant is that my Chinese friends are thoroughly westernised – they drive cars, watch TV, and visit shopping malls. I remember talking to a Thai schoolteacher who is a practising Buddhist. He told me that he read newspapers daily and avidly keeps up to date with the latest ideas in science and culture. Yet, he believes that the world around him is inhabited by spirits, both good and bad. The only computer in his school didn't work, he told me, because it was inhabited by an evil spirit. He was only too well aware that this would come across as bizarre to a westerner steeped in science, but then again, as he informed me, he could not escape his culture.

When I think about the Port Erroll fishermen I think about that Thai schoolteacher. It would be a huge mistake to assume that these fisher folk were rustic or backward. They were reasonably sophisticated people, educated at school, who could resort to using the law, write powerful arguments in letters to newspapers, and make a strong case to a Parliamentary Select Committee. Yet they believed in hundreds of superstitions, many ancient in origin.

Bram Stoker would have realised this after talking to the fishermen. Perhaps this was the origin of the bit in *Dracula* where he contrasts the modern world with the ancient, when Professor van Helsing says, 'All we have to go upon are traditions and superstitions [concerning a belief in vampires]... A year ago which of us would have received such a possibility, in the midst of our scientific, sceptical, matter-of-fact nineteenth century?'

Some of the local fishermen's superstitions may even have got Bram Stoker into the mood for *Dracula*. The Aberdeenshire fishermen, as a folk-lore expert told me, worshipped the Christian God onshore yet believed in 'Neptune' while at sea. That is, they sensed a supernatural presence in the sea, although it was something they feared rather than worshipped.

According to Peter Anson, who wrote several books about the fishing industry of NE Scotland, this belief was universal among fishermen throughout Europe. In Port Erroll it was taboo for fishermen to mention anything to do with the Christian faith while out at sea. Words such as minister or church could not be uttered; and should someone unthinkingly do so, the others would shout 'cauld iron', whereby the men rushed to touch an iron object, typically a horseshoe nailed to a mast.

Could Bram Stoker have thus been inspired to imagine a pagan entity inhabiting the sea as a proxy for the monstrous behaviour of Count Dracula?

Now, here's a thing - Bram liked to link his descriptions of the sea and the coast to the supernatural. Telling are the comments made by Annie Cruickshank, James Cruickshank's wife, who was still alive in the 1970s. She was interviewed by several journalists at the time including James Drummond. In one interview she said, 'I remember Bram Stoker very well. I first met him in 1898 when I was working in the post office at Cruden Bay. He was a burly Irishman with a beard – very jovial, not at all like the characters in his books. He told us he got his inspiration from the cliffs, rocks, sand and sea around Cruden Bay.'

And when Bram describes the coastal scenery around Cruden Bay, he frequently adds a supernatural vibe. Some examples:

**The Watter's Mou'** - a deeply-incised sea gorge near Slains Castle which provides the outlet for the stream known as the Back Burn. In Stoker's novel *The Watter's Mou'* (1895) Willie 'pointed to where a line of sharp rocks rose between the billows on the south side of the inlet. Truly, it was a fearful-looking place to be dashed on, for the great waves broke on the rocks with a loud roaring, and even in the semi-darkness they could see the white lines as the waters poured down to leeward in the wake of the heaving wave. The white cluster of rocks looked like a ghostly mouth opened to swallow whatever might come in touch.' [*The Watter's Mou'* (1895)]

The Watter's Mou'. 'The white cluster of rocks looked like a ghostly mouth...'

**Cruden Bay -** 'If Cruden Bay is to be taken figuratively as a mouth, with the sand hills for soft palate, and the green Hawklaw as the tongue, the rocks which work the extremities are its teeth.' [*The Mystery of the Sea* (1902)]

**The Skares** – the deadly reefs extending offshore for half a mile from the coast near Whinnyfold. 'Did the sea hold its dead where they fell, its floor around the Skares would be whitened with their bones, and new islands could build themselves with the piling wreckage.' [*The Mystery of the Sea* (1902)] And, in a chapter later in the book, he describes a procession of the ghosts of the drowned sailors as they emerge from the Skares.

Dacre Stoker, great-grand nephew of Bram, pointing at the Skares.

Something else too: it seems that when Bram Stoker talked to the fishermen of Port Erroll he annoyed Adam Drummond for some reason. In James Drummond's archive are notes from a story written by his grandfather with the title *Wulsey's Return*. Unfortunately the complete story itself is missing. Here are James Drummond's jottings from it - Bram Stoker is here referred to as 'Soker':

```
ADAM DRUMMOND

WULSEY'S RETURN


'....encountered Soker, a worthless creature  .. morbid
preoccupation with black superstitions  . death and funeral
customs...

"..he (Soker)  ..spends altogether too much time in graveyards.."

".. peculiar fascination for ghoulish stories  "
```

Also in the archive is what I believe to be a misplaced page from *Wulsey's Return*; the rest of the story is missing. Here is this page transcribed in both the Doric original and in an English translation:

[Original] 'He said things he sudna said, an' he wad tak' a' back the nicht, fur he believes nae word o't.'

'Fu than,' said Wully, 'dis he no' tak it back? Fan a man's vrang he sud own til't.'

'Fu did ye no' tak' back yon? - ye ken fat a mean,' said Wulsey, as Wulley got red in the face and shifted his legs uneasily.

'Oh weel,' said Wulley, 'I couldna bring my min' til't - Soker's sic a peer craterie.'

'Jist that,' said Wulsey, 'But that was pride on your pairt, an' it's jist the same faut' at hinners the man at we're speakin' aboot. Fyles ae faut taks us into tribble, syne fan we wad like to get decent kin' anither faut keps us.'

'I wadna say but fat ye're vricht Wulsey" said Wulley humbly, 'But fat wad ye purpose to dae?'

'Lat them alane,' said Wulsey. 'The wye ye dae wi' the loonies fan their quarrellin', an' be as kin' an' dacent to them baith as ye can an' it'l a' come vricht.'

Turning to the minister, Wulsey said: 'Fur yer ain sake, Sir, dinna meddle wi't eenoo, an' tak care o' the man fa says he's yer best frien' in the Ward, an' alloos at they'r baith vricht, fur they'r baith vrang. Haud to that. They want to fin' oot fat side ye tak.'

Whereupon both rose to go, and, as they parted at the door, Wulley said: 'I'm thinkin' syne ye'l see 'at Wulsey's vricht. He aye beats me fan he taks me yon wye.'

[English] 'He said things he should not have said, and he would take everything back tonight, because he doesn't believe a word of it.'

'How then,' said Wully, 'does he not take it back? When a man's wrong he should own up to it.'

'How did you not take back that? - you know what I mean,' said Wulsey, as Wulley got red in the face and shifted his legs uneasily.

'Oh well,' said Wulley, 'I couldn't bring my mind to it - Soker's such a poor creature.'

'Just that,' said Wulsey. 'But that was pride on your part, and it's just the same fault that hinders the man that we're speaking about. While one fault takes us into trouble, then when we would like to get civil another fault holds us up.'

'Perhaps you are right Wulsey,' said Wulley humbly, 'but what would you suggest to do?'

'Let things alone,' said Wulsey, 'The way you do with the young boys when they are quarrelling, and be as kind and decent to them both as you can and it will all come right.'

Turning to the minister, Wulsey said: 'For your own sake, Sir, do not meddle with it just now, and take care of the man who says he's your best friend in the Ward, and allow that they are both right, because they are both wrong. Hold to that. They want to find out what side you take.'

Whereupon both rose to go, and, as they parted at the door, Wulley said: 'I'm thinking then you will see that Wulsey's right. He always beats me when he takes me that way.'

Adam Drummond's original typescript mentioning 'Soker' is shown here.

> ment in a day. Its no like the scaw 'at ye can scrape aff yer boat, it's mair like a twist in her keel at she took fan she was bigget. Ye canna tak it oot, fur its in the stick, but ye can guide fan the boat jibs. He said things he sudna said, an' he wad tak' a' back the nicht, fur he believes nae word o't." "Fu than" said Wully "dis he no' tak it back? Fan a man's vrang he sud own tilt." "Fu did ye no' tak' back yon? - ye ken fat a mean" said Wulsey, as Wulley got red in the face and shifted his legs uneasily.
>
> "Oh weel" said Wulley, "i couldna bring my min' til't - Soker's sic a peer craterie." "Jist that" said Wulsey, "but that was pride on your pairt, an' it's jist the same faut'at hinners the man at we're speakin' aboot. Fyles ae faut taks us into tribble, syne fan we wad like to get oot dacent kin' anither faut keps us." "I wadna say but fat ye're vricht Wulsey" said Wulley humbly, "But fat wad ye purpose to dae?" "Lat them alane" said Wulsey. "The wye ye dae wi' the loonies fan their quarrellin', an' be as kin' an' dacent to them baith as ye can an' it'l a' come vricht." Turning to the Minister, Wulsey said: "Fur yer ain sake, Sir, dinna meddle wi't eenoo, an' tak care o' the man fa says he's yer best frien' in the Ward, an' alloos at they'r baith vricht, fur they'r baith vrang. Haud to that. They want to fin' oot fat side ye tak."
>
> Whereupon both rose to go, and, as they parted at the door, Wulley said: "I'm thinkin' syne ye'l see 'at Wulsey's vricht. He aye beats me fan he taks me yon wye."

It appears that Wulley and 'Soker' had got into an argument about some matter. Wulley describes 'Soker' as a poor craterie - a poor creature – a phrase just a touch rude in Doric because it hints that the person described is feeble or less than a human being. And the minister is also told 'take care of the man who says he's your best friend in the Ward'. 'Take care' in this context meaning 'watch out for'. It hints that 'Soker', an affable man on the surface, is not to be trusted.

So what happened here? I don't know, although it is possible that Adam Drummond was uncomfortable that Bram Stoker had been asking the fisher folk about their superstitions. Furthermore, he may have considered that he was responsible for the spiritual mindset of the fisher folk, and that Bram was distracting them from focussing on the Christian God by his keen interest in their non-Christian beliefs.

Sometime later, when Bram Stoker wrote The Mystery of the Sea, from 1900 or so (and after having written *Dracula* in the village), he discussed the ancient pagan influence on the festival known as Lammas-tide, the traditional start of the annual harvest on the first of August:

> Doubtless I could have found out all I wanted from some of the ministers of the various houses of religion which hold in Cruden; but I was not wishful to make public, even so far, the mystery which was closing around me. My feeling was partly a saving sense of humour, or the fear of ridicule, and partly a genuine repugnance to enter upon the subject with anyone who might not take it as seriously as I could wish.

Ouch!

Dacre Stoker holding Bram Stoker's copy of *Dracula* in Cruden Bay.

## 5. WHAT HAPPENED AFTER 1895

Adam Drummond left Port Erroll Congregational Church in 1895 to take up a post as the minister of the Congregational Church in Macduff, a fishing village on the Banffshire coast. From there he went to Wick, where he died in 1912, age 63. His son, James Craigie Drummond, became the minister of the Peterhead Congregational Church, and his grandson, James Adam Drummond, was the vice-principal of Craigie and Aberdeen Colleges of Education, an author, and a journalist. James Drummond was fascinated by Bram Stoker's time in Cruden Bay, writing several articles on the topic and fronting a TV documentary on the subject in 1995. He died on October 24, 1997.

Devotion to the Christian faith in Cruden Bay lessened with time. Already by 1912, the Reverend Adam MacKay, Minister of the Cruden Parish Church, was writing about 'the problem of religious indifference'. Symptoms included spending 'Sunday on the golf course' or loafing 'in idleness at home'. He adds somewhat mournfully that: 'Religion by compulsion may have an unattractive sound. I admit it. But surely to insist that a man will show evidence that he puts himself under wholesome discipline, and has a mind superior to selfishness and gross pleasure, is elementary wisdom.'

The local economy around Port Erroll was in decline by 1912. Agriculture was in the doldrums; prices having collapsed because of cheap grain imports from abroad. The result was that 'each year there is an exodus from the agricultural to the colonies or elsewhere'. And neither was the local granite industry prospering. The local granite had become more expensive to extract, and was already in competition with imports from abroad. Fortunately the local brickworks still gave employment to thirty men.

By 1912, the Port Erroll fishing industry had substantially diminished; Reverend MacKay noting that fishing 'is only profitable when conducted on a large scale by trawlers and steam drifters'. In consequence: 'line-fishing is almost nil; and the conditions of the net-fishing industry, which compel the fishermen to employ steam drifters, and to live in the big centres of population, are rapidly denuding the parish of its fisher population'. He adds that: 'Like the rest of the fishing villages along the coast, Port Erroll is rapidly becoming depleted. Fishing is now carried out locally merely by small boats; and the harbour is seldom used by ships of any size, except when bringing in coals, or when taking away a cargo of grain, etc.' It was the huge misfortune of the fishermen from Port Erroll to have suffered the human cost of an early man-made ecological catastrophe: the rapid decline of fishing stocks in the North Sea.

That was 1912. Two years later World War I started, and when it ended in 1918 the population of Port Erroll was devastated. Inside the front door of the Congregational Church is 'The Roll of Honour', Cruden Bay's war memorial.

| | | | |
|---|---|---|---|
| Morgan, J.W. R.N.R. | Whinnyfold | Hay, William. R.N.R. | Whinnyfold |
| Forman, Geo. | do. | Hay, John do. | do. |
| Robertson, William | R.N.R.T | | 5. Green St |
| Robertson, John. W. | Skipper R.N.R. | | 5. Ward St |
| Robertson, Alexander | R.N.R.T. | | 20. Harbour St |
| Robertson, James | do. | | do. |
| Robertson, Thomas | do. | | 6. New Block |
| Robertson, William | R.N.D. | Died in Action | 14. Main St |
| Robertson, Adam. L. | Gordon Hrs. | | do. |
| Robertson, George | do | Killed 1918 | do. |
| Robertson, Alex ndr | R.S.F | do. do. | do. |
| Robertson, James. C. | A.&.S.H | | do. |
| Ross, William | R.N.D. | | do |
| Ross, Alexander | R.F. | | Aulton Road |
| Ross, Thomas | R.E. | | do. |
| Ross, Frank | | | do. |
| Ross, Jesse | Gordon Hrs. | Wounded 1918 | do. |
| Sangster, James | R.A.M.C. | | Cruden Bay Hotel |
| Sim, Alexander | M.G.C. | Twice W'd. 1917-18 | 5 Hay St |
| Sim, Henry | Gordon Hrs. | Died | Links Cottage |
| Simpson, Jas. C. | A.S.C. | | do. |
| Smith, Frank. H. | K.R.R. | Twice W'd. 1917-18 | 29. Main St |
| Smith, Frank. G. | M.G.C. | | 11 Main St |

From the Roll of Honour, Port Erroll 1914-1918.

And like many towns and villages up and down the land, the list of names of the killed, wounded, or gassed is long and depressing. What makes the memorial so poignant is that the addresses of the men are also listed. Those living today can look at the list and gasp in horror that two, three, or more names from the house they live in are listed on the memorial. One house in Main Street has five names on the list. Needless to say, economic activity in and around Port Erroll plummeted even further at the end of the war.

By 1928, there were six motor boats working out of Port Erroll Harbour with crews of three or four men. The main activity today at the harbour is creel fishing for lobster and crabs; fishing not quite having died out.

Thus came about the collapse of fishing villages in Aberdeenshire. Up to the end of the nineteenth century there were sixty-three fishing villages along 120 miles of coast in

NE Scotland; many with over a hundred fisherfolk living in them, and several with over 300. And then line-fishing became uneconomic because of the overfishing of the North Sea. Whole villages disappeared. For example the village Bram Stoker knew as Oldcastle, which had grown up around the ruins of Old Slains Castle, was abandoned in 1900 when the inhabitants moved to Aberdeen. Today there are no obvious indications that there had ever been a village there.

In this context, Adam Drummond's stories provide a glimpse into a way of life before it disappeared forever; that of an Aberdeenshire fishing community looking out for each other with intense human closeness.

And at the other end of the social scale, Charles Gore Hay, the earl Bram Stoker knew, was eventually overwhelmed by money problems. From 1900, Slains Castle was rented out as a high-class summer holiday home; an early visitor, if not the first, was Lord Baden-Powell, founder of the Scout movement. And in 1916 the castle was sold to a shipping magnate, and then sold again. It was subsequently bought by a demolition contractor from Dundee who then stripped the lead and slates from the roof and advertised masonry and fittings from the castle for sale. By this time the earl had abandoned the area to live in England. In his absence, Port Erroll was renamed Cruden Bay in 1924.

Cruden Bay Railway Station opened in 1897, with the luxury hotel opening two years later. The hotel was profitable up until about 1910, but then the income from the resort became marginal to poor thereafter. The summer season was short and the hotel too far away from London; the real Brighton being much closer for its inhabitants to visit than the 'Brighton of the North'. The hotel fell into disuse at the end of World War II, and was eventually demolished in 1953. The railway fared no better; the station burned down in 1931 and was not replaced. The railway line itself was last used in 1945, with the tracks removed in 1950.

*Dracula*, partly written in Port Erroll, was eventually highly successful, but did not make its author much money in his lifetime. When the Lyceum Theatre closed down after Henry Irving died in 1905, Bram Stoker was out of work and desperate to find income other than from the minor royalties he received from the sale of his books. Seriously ill on his last visit to the area in 1910, he died in 1912.

## Salads, Sauces, &c.

### SALAD.

(Mrs PIRIE, Bank House, Lonmay).

Wash and pick two heads of lettuce. Shred them, and add the white of a hard-boiled egg cut in rings. Pound the yolk. Add a little salt, a large teaspoonful of made mustard, one breakfastcupful of cream, and a little vinegar. Mix well. Pour over the lettuce, and turn over the whole a few times wtih a spoon and fork. If liked a few slices of tomato may be added.

### THE "DRACULA" SALAD.

(Mrs BRAM STOKER, 26 St George's Square, London, S.W.)

Arrange alternate slices of ripe tomatoes, and ripe, purple, egg-shaped plums in dish, and dress with oil and vinegar French dressing.

### BREAD SAUCE.

(Mrs J. SMITH, Easterton, Peterhead).

½ pint milk.  2 cloves.
1 small onion.  2 oz. bread crumbs.
Pepper and salt.  1 oz. butter.

Stick the cloves in the onion. Put the milk in a saucepan. Add the onion, and set at the side of stove for half an hour. Warm it, but do not boil. Shake out the onion and add the crumbs, butter, salt, and a good pinch of pepper. Stir until the bread crumbs have absorbed the milk.

Florence Stoker's recipe for The "Dracula" Salad in *Cruden Recipe's and Wrinkles*, compiled for Cruden Parish Church in 1912.

Were there any success stories amidst all the gloom? Yes. Cruden Bay Golf Course survived the nationalisation of the railways at the end of World War II, but only just. Appalled by the government's plan to sell it for agricultural land, the owner of the Kilmarnock Arms Hotel gathered a consortium of businessmen together and bought the golf course. Today it is regularly listed amongst the top hundred courses in the world.

Florence Stoker became rich from *Dracula* when the 1931 film of the novel starring Bela Lugosi was made. She was paid royalties from what proved a wildly popular film. And, thereafter, a book written in an Aberdeen fishing village became world famous.

Finally, some breaking news: three days ago as of writing - the Cruden Bay (Port Erroll) Congregational Church held its last ever service on Sunday, 26th February, 2023. The congregation now made their decision together; the building and the land will be donated to the Cruden Bay Community Association to be used for community activities; a decision which has gained the gratitude of the entire village.

Cruden Bay Congregational Church, February 2023.

# REFERENCES

Peter F. Anson, 1965. *Fisher Folklore, Old Customs, Taboos and Superstitions Among Fisher Folk, Especially in Brittany and Normandy, and on the East Coast Of Scotland.* The Faith Press London.

'H. B.' *Letters From the Crimea, During the Years 1854 and 1855.* Emily Faithful. London.

James R. Coull, *The Sea Fisheries of Scotland : a historical geography.* John Donald, Edinburgh.

James Dalgarno, 1896. *From The Brig O' Balgownie To The Bullers O' Buchan: With The Golf Courses.* W. Jolly & Sons, Albany Press, Aberdeen.

James Drummond, *Bram Stoker's Cruden Bay*, Scots Magazine, April 1976.

S. P. Duncan / J.J. Waterman, 1989. *Postal Histories – The Postal Service in the Parish of Cruden.* Unpublished document in the files of Jim Gentle.

Jim Gentle, *The Street Names Of Cruden Bay.* Copy held in Cruden Bay Public Library.

Emily Gerard, 1885. *Transylvanian Superstitions.* The Nineteenth Century (Vol. 18), London, July-December 1885, pp. 130-150.

Walter Gregor, 1874. *An Echo of the Olden Times in the North of Scotland.* John Menzies.

Walter Gregor, 1881. *Notes on the Folk-Lore of the North-East of Scotland.* Elliot Stock, London.

James Leatham, 1937. *Fisher folk of the North-East .* Second edition. Deveron Press.

Harry Ludlam, 1977. *A Biography of Bram Stoker Creator of Dracula.* New English Library.

Harry Ludlam, 2000. *My Quest for Bram Stoker.* Dracula Press. New York.
Adam Mackay, 1912. Cruden and its Ministers. P. Scrogie, Peterhead.

J. M. McPherson, 1929. *Primitive Beliefs in the North-East of Scotland.* Longmans, Green And Co., London, New York, Toronto.

James Miller, 1999. *Salt in the Blood.* Canongate, Edinburgh.

Mike Shepherd, 2018. *When Brave Men Shudder; the Scottish origins of Dracula.* Wild Wolf Publishing.

Mike Shepherd and Dacre Stoker, 2021. *Slains Castle's Secret History.* Wild Wolf

Publishing.

Bram Stoker, 1895. *The Watter's Mou'*, A. Constable & Co., Westminster.

Bram Stoker, 1897. *Dracula*. William Heinemann, London.

Bram Stoker, 1902. *The Mystery of the Sea*. William Heinemann, London.

Bram Stoker, *The Crooken Sands*, in *Dracula's Guest*. 1914 George Routledge and Sons.

*Guide to Cruden Bay and Neighbourhood.* The Rosemount Press, Aberdeen. 1908.

Newspapers: Buchan Observer, Press and Journal, Peterhead Sentinel

Printed in Great Britain
by Amazon